folktales are forever

"**Folktales are Forever** is a delightful contribution to the Nigerian literary heritage. Well-nigh inexhaustible, the treasury of our folklore is in passionate search of transmutation from oral to written form. Efe Farinre has deftly captured the cadences of the spoken word and the haunting lyrical music that sometimes transcends the narrative, taking on a life of its own. Children and parents owe her a debt of gratitude.

"The folktales are drawn from folklore, but the author's poetic voice, rich characterization, evocative ambience, and robust sense of humor make **Folktales are Forever** a distinct work of literature. A whole generation of Nigerian children grew up watching Tales By Moonlight. Their own children now have the blessing of experiencing the heights of their imagination as Efe Farinre leads them into one adventure after another, using these tales of humans and animals in such an engaging manner to entertain and teach. Thank God this is Volume One. We who are grandparents and grandchildren, parents and children, cry, "Author, Author, give us Volume Two!""

— **Dr. Victoria C. Ezeokoli,**
 Creator of TALES BY MOONLIGHT ,
 Pioneer Director of Programmes,
 Nigerian Television Authority

"These interesting folktales are skilfully retold in a unique and charming style. Children and adults will find them instructive and entertaining."

— **Akachi Adimora-Ezeibgo,**
   Writer & Professor of English,
   University of Lagos, Nigeria

« Le recueil de contes intitule *Folktales are Forever* *écrit par Efe Farinre est un véritable chef d'œuvre. Ces contes, tirés de l'immense répertoire des textes oraux des populations nigérianes jouent un grand rôle pédagogique pour les enfants pour apprendre de manière ludique les réalités historiques, sociologiques, linguistiques, de leur environnement. La mise par écrit de ces contes et légendes, Efe Farinre triple l'effet de ce travail patrimonial par la musique de Gbenga Ezekiel. En ce qui concerne les dessins, ils donnent aux textes une dimension encore plus onirique et élargissent l'horizon du voyage. Ainsi conçu le recueil sollicite son public par la vue, l'ouïe et l'imagination. Il l'introduit dans un monde animalier et végétal ou toute la nature parlait avec l'homme.* »

"The collection of stories entitled **Folktales are Forever** written by Efe Farinre is a true masterpiece. These tales, drawn from the vast repertory of oral texts of the Nigerian people play an important educational role for children. It teaches them in a fun way, historical, sociological and linguistic facts of their country. In writing these tales, Efe Farinre triples the effect of this work of heritage with music, by Gbenga Ezekiel and illustrations, which give the stories a more dreamlike quality and broaden their horizon to readers. **Folktales are Forever** attracts its audience through sight, sound and imagination. It introduces readers to a world of animals and plants, where nature speaks with man."

— **Professor Nouréini Remi Tidjani-Serpos, Ancien President du Conseil Executif de l'UNESCO, Assistant Director General (Africa Department), UNESCO (Retired), President, The Panafrican Foundation for Cultural Development (FONPADEC)**

"**Folktales are Forever** is an artistic packaging of folktales from our age-long culture of moonlight gatherings. Written in simple, easily digestive language, it is as innocent as its target audience, though I would also recommend it for adults. The storybook has revealed Efe's voyage in the creative world. Steeped in our local culture and heritage, **Folktales are Forever** underscores the essence of traditional value and is very entertaining."

— **Jimi Solanke, Actor, Playright, Poet, Folk Artiste, Creator of STORYLAND**

"**Folktales are Forever** is a long overdue, but welcome, addition to the world of children's literature in Nigeria.

Efe Farinre has told these folktales with simplicity, humour and skill. With vibrant illustrations, enjoyable songs and rhymes, she takes you on a magical trip to folktale land where animals assume human form. These charming stories should appeal to all children."

— **Stephanie Ofonagoro, Educationist,
   Rtd. Headmistress, University of Lagos Women
   Society Nursery School**

"**Folktales are Forever**, a work that is so dear to my heart, brings back memories of those nights in the village growing up […] and gathering under the tree at night for the tales by moonlight. And at the end of each night there was the presentation of the good and bad consequences of the story. Iya Agba—loosely translated as Granny, the story teller—would let us know the implications of choosing our paths in life either the right way or the bad, drawing examples from the stories. And I can still remember that the tortoise of those legends always trying to be wiser than all and always paying the price for taking the fast lane."

— **Adebowale Ibidapo Adefuye (1947 - 2015),
   Professor of History and former Ambassador of
   Nigeria to the United States of America**

"Our people say, *the words of the elders are the words of wisdom.* Folktales and folksongs were created by our forefathers to guide us in charting the right course in life. As I have dedicated my life to preserving "our good old days", by spreading Nigerian traditional arts & crafts all over the world in contemporary ways, **Folktales are Forever** will also preserve an important part of our rich cultural heritage."

— **Chief (Mrs.) Nike Okundaye, Managing Director/ CEO Nike Centre for Art & Culture, Nigeria, Owner & Curator, Nike Art Galleries, Nigeria**

"Folktales are a universal phenomenon: they are found in all cultures of the world, serving various purposes for the social, ethical and intellectual life of the people who own them. Folktales are more resounding in the original language/dialect of its owners: but this author, Efe Farinre, has succeeded summarily in rendering them in English Language with remarkable accuracy and literary finesse.

The inclusion of the songs attached to the tales (These are usually referred to as "folktales songs") calls us back vividly, to the lively atmosphere with which these tale-lessons imprinted their ethical, intellectual and civic doctrines in our young minds in those days."

— **Anthony V.E. Mereni, Professor of Musicology & Music Therapy, University of Lagos**

"A book like **Folktales are Forever** meets the needs of Nigerians who are dispersed all over the world. They want to share folktales they grew up on with their children, and this book, with its accessible language, will be enjoyed by children and adults. I like that the stories harken back to the simple morals of truth. For example, the first story shows that though we are never satisfied, God has made us perfect; we always seek to be different, yet God has made us perfect as we are."

— **Joke Silva, Award-Winning Actor,**
 Co-Founder, Lufodo Group & Director of Studies,
 Lufodo Academy of Performing Arts

"Am I not the saviour of the animal kingdom?"

"This question from the story of the Tortoise and the Drum, a story I was lucky to be exposed to as I grew up (in the comfort of culturally relevant narrations), brought a flood of memories to me, and a question: in an age of endless remakes of Snow-white, Cinderella, Beauty and the Beast, why haven't we had re-inventions of our folktales, of our narratives?

What Efe Farinre has done here is to present a timeless gift to a new generation. This gift is the confidence of perspective, the advantage of history, and a tool to engage the world as they confront narratives from places and climes that do not put them front and centre."

— **Chude Jideonwo, Managing Partner of RED and**
 Editor-in-Chief, Y / YNaija.com

"**Folktales are Forever** is an outstanding book of cultural relevance for our children and generations yet unborn. Efe has documented a critical part of our folklore for posterity."
— **Bolanle Austen-Peters, Founder, Terra Kulture**

"In **Folktales are Forever**, Efe Farinre recaptures with gusto the real world of the African past where the traditional narrator/ performer was, for the audience, an educator, philosopher, and counsellor who entertained as he/she instructed and endeavoured to make the values and beliefs portrayed in the tales come alive. Folktales were sources of raw African values and through them the young were led to appreciate the basic ideas of life, a community's fundamental values, their systems of personal relationships and sense of humour. Farinre retells these stories with amazing charm and delightful lucidity. In **Folktales are Forever**, the reader will enjoy humorous timeless African stories whose wisdom and messages transcend the boundaries of race, ethnicity, and tongue. It should be on every shelf and kitchen table!"
— **Ernest N. Emenyonu, Professor of Africana Studies, Editor, African Literature Today, University of Michigan-Flint**

folktales are forever

volume one

Efe Farinre

Narrative
Landscape
Press

For information regarding permission, write to
info@folktalesareforever.com

Published by
Narrative Landscape Press Limited
9, Odunlami Street, Anthony Village, Lagos, Nigeria.
07014522083, 09090554406 - 7
contact@narrativelandscape.com
www. narrativelandscape.com

A catalogue record for this book is available from
the National Library of Nigeria.

ISBN (paperback): 978-978-957-920-4
ISBN (eBook): 978-978-957-922-8

Music by Gbenga Ezekiel
Illustrations and Cover Art by Babajide Olusanya
Book Layout and Cover Design by AI's Fingers

Contents

A Note From The Author

Dear Reader,

I am so glad to share this collection of Nigerian folktales with you.

When my family moved to the U.S. in 2010, my daughters wanted me to tell them "Nigerian stories" every night. Whenever I started one, the common response was, "Grandma already told us that story; don't you know any other one?" We had to agree that it was okay to relay the same stories their grandma had told them, as I really wasn't "copying" her, but sharing the stories my grandma had told me.

Once I had told them all the folktales I knew at the time, I started asking around for more. What

I thought would be easy, surprisingly turned out to be rather difficult. Only a few people from the young to the old could recall folktales from their ethnicity in detail.

It dawned on me that if not properly documented, we Nigerians were fast losing a unique part of our culture.

In a casual conversation, I shared my concerns with my husband and brother in September, 2010. Our discussion led to the importance and urgency of putting together a comprehensive collection of Nigerian folktales. They said to me, "If it bothers you, rather than talking about it, do something about it." And so I put pen to paper and the title *Folktales are Forever* popped up!

Folktales depend on us to stay alive. Folktales that have lived this long should continue to outlive generations upon generations, to last forever.

The stories in *Folktales are Forever* are told across many ethnic groups in Nigeria in different versions. In retelling them here, the language has been kept simple so as to appeal to every age group across the globe – older children will be able to read, understand, enjoy and also retell them, while the inner child in adults will come alive as they also enjoy reading these stories and sharing them with younger children. While the plots of the stories have remained unaltered to maintain their authenticity, the stories have been retold to address both "ancient & modern values".

The English translations of the folk songs that are part of some of the stories have been included in *Folktales are Forever*. In order to preserve their tunes, the music scores and tonic solfas of these folk songs have been provided by Gbenga Ezekiel.

Traditionally in Nigerian villages, adults and children sit under the moonlight while folktales are told, mostly by an "old sage". Folktales are told not only to amuse but also to teach morals. It is a time of fun and relaxation. The story-teller creates more excitement by the words spoken just before telling the folktale. Starting off stories this way has been imbibed when Nigerians tell them in English. It is common for the story-teller to begin by saying, "story, story", the response to which is "story" and then, "once upon a time", and the response is "time, time". And at the end of a folktale, the morals of the story are discussed among the listeners. *Folktales are*

Forever brings you this same enriching experience and in upholding our story-telling culture, after enjoying each reading, do ponder and share the values that they teach.

On the book cover are the *Folktales are Forever* WAZOBIA Mascots. The Tortoise on the left is named Wasibi, the Tortoise in the middle is named Zonan and the Tortoise on the right is named Biaebea. "**Wa** sibi", "**Zo** nan" and "**Bia** ebea" mean "come here" in Nigeria's three major languages of Yoruba, Hausa and Igbo respectively. Our WAZOBIA Mascots beckon you to *Folktales are Forever* for an invaluable cultural experience.

Read, enjoy and share!

Efe Farinre

1

Chimpanzee and its Human Features

All the animals in the kingdom had one wish: they wanted to be more like humans. This wish sometimes made them sad and gloomy.

Dog often wondered how it would feel to grow his own crops and cook his own meals. Cat imagined lifting a bowl of warm milk to her mouth and gulping it down. Snake dreamt of having legs to walk on and hands to reach for food. Lion imagined himself speaking in a rich and captivating voice to a large audience. Chimpanzee, when he looked at his reflection in the river, saw himself dressed in human ceremonial attire.

One day, the Creator visited the animals and was surprised to see them looking unhappy. "Why the sad faces?" he asked.

The animals looked down and didn't respond.

"Come, Lion, Snake, Goat, Hippopotamus, Leopard, Goose," the Creator called. "Come, all of you. Tell me what is going on. What can I do to make you happy again?"

Reluctantly, the animals opened up to the Creator and told him they didn't like how they looked, that they wished they were more like the humans. The Creator listened to them, and after they had spoken he was quiet for some time. Then he said with a sigh, "Each of you is perfect just the way you are."

The animals looked at themselves and shook their heads. They told the Creator they didn't like how he had made them; they began to tell him how he should have made them. Fish said she would have preferred to have legs. Frog said he would have been better as a prince. Horse said he would have loved to be a rider. Cow said she should have been made slim. Butterfly said she should have been made plump. The white sheep wanted to be black and the black sheep wanted to be white! On and on the animals went, complaining and pleading with the Creator to make them more like the humans.

The Creator felt sad and sorry for them. "I have heard you," he said. "I will do as you all have asked. You must all go to the middle of the forest at mid-day, exactly seven days from today. There, you will find a potion in a big clay pot. Rub this potion on your bodies and you will look exactly the way you like. But you must hurry as the potion will dry up very quickly."

The animals were jubilant. Some of them wanted to go looking for the potion immediately. They were so happy that they began a fiesta in celebration of their upcoming change. They took turns hosting one another for the morning, afternoon and evening meals. Each animal tried to outdo the other with large servings of delicious delicacies and drinks. All day and all night, they celebrated. Many were even too excited to sleep. They played their drums, blew their flutes, danced, and ate so much that they did not realise when the week ended and the next one began.

At sunset on the seventh day, Cock suddenly remembered he had not crowed since the merry-making began. He counted the days and in dismay realised it was the seventh day. He looked around at all the animals lost in the joy of the moment, and decided to get their attention the only way he knew. Cock ran up to the roof of the tallest house and crowed with all his might.

"Kukurukoo!"

Immediately, the music ceased, and the dancing halted. In the animal kingdom, anytime Cock crowed unexpectedly, the animals knew that very important news was about to be shared. So when they heard his crow, they ran to where Cock stood and looked up at him.

"What's the news?"

"What's going on?

"Did something happen?"

"Is there an emergency?"

"Are we safe?"

Cock looked down at them and yelled, "Fellow animals, it is the seventh day!"

The animals looked at one another, then up at Cock. "What do you mean it's the seventh day?" They didn't know what he was talking about.

Cock yelled louder, "It is the seventh day!"

Then, slowly, one after the other, the animals remembered and they began to panic. They ran around in confusion and asked one another what to do. They remembered what the Creator had told them and wondered if it was too late to get to the potion. Lion, taking control of the situation, roared and instructed all the animals to head as fast as they could to the middle of the forest before the potion dried up.

Snail asked Lion to put him on his back, but Lion said, "I am about to run faster than I ever have and you will definitely fall off my back."

Snake pleaded with Horse to allow him wrap himself around one of his legs, but Horse said, "You may fall off while I am galloping and I will crush you."

Lizard asked Tiger to let him sit on top of his

head, but Tiger said, "Lizard, your tail may cover my eyes and I will go in the wrong direction."

The animals did not help one another. They all wanted to get to the potion before it dried up.

Chimpanzee looked at all the others as they raced towards the middle of the forest and reasoned that he could get there fastest by swinging from tree to tree. As he was about to reach for the nearest branch, Tortoise stopped him and asked if he would carry him on his back.

"You will be too heavy for me, Tortoise," said Chimpanzee, "Wait behind and I will bring back some potion for you."

Chimpanzee swung from this tree to that tree and from that tree to the other tree. He moved faster than the other animals because he had no obstacles in his way. The other animals, on the other hand, had to run through the bush and swim across the river, brushing and pushing past one another in their haste.

Chimpanzee arrived at the meeting spot first. He quickly found the clay pot with the potion in it almost dried up. "Better something than nothing," was his thought as he quickly began to rub some potion on his hands, face, and feet. He was about to rub what was remaining on his body when he caught his reflection in a puddle beside him. His hands, face and feet were already changed. He paused. Suddenly, he didn't want to be like the humans anymore. Somewhere in his mind the words of the Creator began to echo over and over.

"Each of you is perfect just the way you are. Each of you is perfect just the way you are."

It dawned on Chimpanzee that the only reason he got to the meeting point first was because he could swing from tree to tree. "If I didn't have my long arms and limbs, I would have had to walk," he

thought. His thoughts drifted to his fellow animals: His dear friend, Tortoise, never got hurt while playing because of his hard shell. Cock's crow woke them up each morning and alerted them to emergencies. Lion's roar scared away hunters. Elephant's trunk was a swing for the little animals to play on. Giraffe used his height to help the animals get fruits from the tallest trees. Hippo was huge enough to put some animals on his back when they needed to cross the river.

Chimpanzee was still thinking when the other animals arrived.

"Wait," he shouted. "The Creator is right!"

But the animals, desperate for the potion, didn't hear him as they rushed towards the clay pot. Chimpanzee jumped up the tree next to him and yelled louder, "The Creator is right!"

This time, the animals stopped and began to look around them. They thought Chimpanzee had said, "The Creator is here."

"Where is the Creator?" they asked. "Your hands, face and feet have changed," they said, looking up and down at Chimpanzee. "Is there any potion left?"

"I said the Creator is right. Each of us is perfect just the way we are," said Chimpanzee. He shared his earlier thoughts with the animals and then asked each of them to think of his or her own uniqueness; the things he or she was good at and how their differences complimented one another. The forest became silent and the potion forgotten as the animals pondered over what Chimpanzee had said.

They looked inwards. They looked at one another. One after the other, they came to the same conclusion: *"Each of us is perfect just the way we are."*

2

How Lion became the King of the Jungle

A long time ago, the animals had no king. They lived together as equals and the animals went about their activities without a leader. Some animals who were particularly skilful or big or strong were respected and consulted when help was needed. Elephant was one of these animals; he was revered for his formidable size. Trees shook when he walked, the ground quaked when he danced, and when he blew through his trunk, birds scattered from the trees. No animal compared to Elephant in stature and in stance, and Elephant knew this.

One day, after thinking about it for a while, Elephant decided that he might as well become king.

"I am bigger than all of you," said Elephant to the other animals. "I am stronger, and I can do anything I want. I hereby demand that you crown me king over all of you."

The animals were not pleased, but Elephant was truly bigger and stronger than them all, so they said nothing.

"My coronation ceremony shall hold in seven days," continued Elephant, "and preparations must start now."

Late at night, some of the animals met secretly to discuss what they would do about Elephant.

"We all know we can't make Elephant king over us," whispered Tiger. "Even without being our king he is already taking advantage of weaker animals. It will only get worse if we make him king."

"I agree," whispered Dog. "Elephant is not compassionate; he can't be our king."

"I agree too," said Parrot, "Elephant is not patient; he can't be our king."

"He is selfish too," said Monkey. "He can't be our king. Once he asked me to harvest all the bananas on his farm and when I took them to him, he didn't offer me any. I worked so hard for him and was not rewarded."

"But if we can't have Elephant as king," said Tiger, "we must have another who can protect us. An animal equally strong but with all the good qualities Elephant lacks."

Slowly, their eyes turned to Lion.

"Yes, Lion has all the qualities," said Owl.

"I agree," said Cock.

"Lion should be king," said Chimpanzee. The animals nodded in agreement. "We shall crown Lion king."

Lion nodded. "I humbly accept this honour," he said, "and I promise to be a worthy king." Then the animals made a plan on how they would go about crowning Lion instead of Elephant.

"I suggest we keep this plan discrete and ensure that Elephant does not get wind of it," said Owl.

The next day, the animals began making preparations for the coronation ceremony as Elephant had ordered. They trimmed the trees, levelled the grass and cleared the grounds. They built a huge and beautiful throne. They worked very hard for six days.

Elephant often came to inspect their work and he would yell, "This is not right! Correct this! This is not good enough for me!" The animals became even more disappointed in him.

On the coronation day, dressed in his best attire, Elephant led the animals in a dance around the jungle. As they danced, Elephant asked the animals to sing:

A o m'ẹ́rin j'ọba	*We shall crown Elephant as King*
Ẹ̀wẹ̀kú Ewẹlẹ	*Ẹ̀wẹ̀kú Ewẹlẹ*[1]
A o m'ẹ́rin j'ọba	*We shall crown Elephant as King*
Ẹ̀wẹ̀kú Ewẹlẹ	*Ẹ̀wẹ̀kú Ewẹlẹ*

As the animals sang, Elephant danced proudly

---

1 Onomatopoeic refrain

towards his throne. The animals had laid a beautiful spread of palm fronds before the throne. Closer and closer to the throne Elephant danced. When Elephant took the last step towards the throne, the palm fronds gave way under his weight and he fell into a pit with a loud crash.

The animals gathered round the pit and watched Elephant struggling to get out. But the pit was so deep that Elephant would be unable to get out without their help. Elephant soon grew tired and began to plead for their help.

"We don't want you as our king," the animals said down to him. "We have chosen Lion to be our king, and we will not help you out of this pit until you agree to accept him as your king."

Finally, exhausted, Elephant agreed to accept Lion as king, and the animals helped him out.

"All hail the king of the jungle," the animals chorused as Lion took to his throne. Elephant and the other animals bowed to him.

Lion roared in response and the entire jungle shook.

"All hail the king of the jungle," the animals chorused again.

3

How Tortoise became Bald

One cool evening, just after the rain, Tortoise set out to visit his parents-in-law. It was a beautiful evening. The leaves on the trees along the path were shining and dripping with the rain. The birds had all come out again, singing as they played in the trees. Tortoise whistled in tune with the birds as he strolled on, avoiding the puddles on his path.

"What a lovely evening," he said to himself as

he walked along. "If Yanrinbo and the young ones were home, it would have been a perfect time for some outdoor family games." He sighed. "Just one more week and they will be back," he murmured as he jumped over another puddle and took the last turn to his in-laws' house.

When Tortoise knocked on the door, his mother-in-law let him in. "You are welcome, my son," she said. "Please come in and make yourself at home." As she led Tortoise inside, she called out to her husband, "Baba Yanrinbo, Tortoise is here to see us."

"Ah! Welcome, my son, I will be with you in a moment," her husband said from somewhere within the house.

When Baba Yanrinbo joined them in the sitting room, he asked after his daughter and grandchildren. "I hope Yanrinbo and the young ones are having a nice time in the next village."

"Oh, yes, they are," replied Tortoise. "I got a message from them yesterday. The young ones are happy to be with their cousins and Yanrinbo is enjoying the company of her sister."

"So you are at home all by yourself," said his

mother-in-law with a smile. "You must miss them a lot."

Tortoise smiled and nodded.

"Well, I hope you've been eating," continued his mother-in-law. "I know with Yanrinbo's absence, you won't be eating as you used to. But not to worry, I am making dinner. You must join us." With that she rose and went into the kitchen.

"You don't want to miss her special yam pottage," added his father-in-law with a knowing smile.

Tortoise smiled back at his father-in-law and said he was not in a hurry; he would be happy to join them for dinner.

Soon, the aroma of his mother-in-law's cooking filled the room and Tortoise's nose began to twitch even as his mouth watered. He was glad when his mother-in-law returned and set bowls of steaming yam pottage, green vegetables and smoked fish before them. Tortoise ate one plate, and then another, and then another.

"Would you like some to take home with you?" asked his mother-in-law.

Feeling a little embarrassed, Tortoise replied

as he licked his lips, "Errr, no, thanks. I think I have had enough."

After the meal, they all went to sit on the verandah to talk and enjoy the cool evening breeze.

"I wonder who will win the race this year," said the father-in-law.

"Hare hopes to beat Antelope this time around," responded Tortoise.

"He has been hoping to do that for many years now," the father-in-law said, laughing.

They shared jokes and talked about the upcoming village games, the building of more market stalls, and the clearing of an additional path to connect their village with the next one. After a while, Tortoise stood up and excused himself. "I would like to use the toilet before I set off home," he said.

"Of course," said his mother-in-law. "You know where it is."

As Tortoise walked back into the house, the aroma of the yam pottage hit him.

"This yam pottage is simply irresistible," Tortoise said to himself as he walked into the toilet.

When he walked out, he was again welcomed by the aroma of the yam pottage. He paused and sniffed. The door to the kitchen was open and Tortoise took a peek inside. He saw the pot on the stove and his mouth watered at the thought of its contents. He looked out towards the verandah where he could still hear his in-laws talking. And then, assured that they were seated, he dashed into the kitchen.

Tortoise only wanted to see if there was any pottage left in the pot. He just wanted to have one last look at the delicious meal before he left the house. When he opened the pot, the aroma wafted straight into his nostrils and Tortoise sighed with longing. He saw the pieces of yam, the red sauce and the fish and knew he had to have some more of the pottage.

"But if I ask for more, they will think I am greedy," Tortoise thought.

He looked behind him towards the verandah again. Satisfied that his in-laws were still out there, he used the big spoon beside the pot to scoop up some pottage. He then began to look desperately around for a container for the food.

Only plates were inside the wooden chest on his right. Cups were what he found in the wooden chest next to the mortar and pestle. When he looked up, he saw a small bowl on a shelf that would be just suitable. He reached for the bowl, but as he did, his hand knocked down a pot cover and it clattered to the floor.

"Tortoise, is that you?" His father-in-law called out. "Are you okay in there?"

Tortoise didn't respond. As he bent quickly to pick up the pot cover, he heard footsteps approaching. He looked at the spoonful of yam pottage in his hand and up again at the bowl on the top-shelf. Tortoise made a quick decision: he took off his cap, emptied the spoonful of yam pottage into it and pulled it back over his head. Hurrying out of the kitchen, he almost bumped into his father-in-law.

"I heard something fall in the kitchen," said his father-in-law, "I was coming to find out what it was. Were you in the kitchen?"

"No, I wasn't in the kitchen. I didn't even hear... I didn't...hear..." Tortoise began to stammer as the hot pottage under his cap began to burn his head.

"Are you all right?" asked his mother-in-law,

who had walked over to them. "Tortoise, you look like you are in pain."

"I... I... am... fine." Tortoise said. A trickle of the hot pottage rolled down his face and Tortoise quickly wiped it.

"What's that running down your face? Is that... red sweat? I wonder if you ate so much that you are sweating yam pottage!" laughed his father-in-law.

"No... It's just sweat... it's the heat... the hot weather... I'll be on my way now," said Tortoise.

But his mother-in-law had seen the reddish sweat too, and now she could smell the pottage on Tortoise. The mother-in-law winked at her husband, just as another drop of reddish sweat trickled down Tortoise's head. Tortoise wiped it off frantically and turned towards the door, more of the pottage leaking from under his cap.

"Oh, wait," said his father-in-law, finally understanding his wife's wink. "You can't go sweating like that. Wait a while to cool off. Mama Yanrinbo, please bring him some water."

Now that the in-laws knew what Tortoise had done, and what the hot pottage was doing to him, they decided to delay him as punishment.

"I am not very thirsty. Let me just head on home," Tortoise said hurriedly.

"Oh no, my dear, sit down for just a minute," said his mother-in-law, pulling Tortoise down to a chair. "There is this new board game I was hoping we could all play together."

The father-in-law brought down a rectangular wooden box and began to tell Tortoise the rules of the game. By now Tortoise was almost turning red with pain. He knew he couldn't take it much longer. "I have a long day tomorrow and I really need to go to bed early," Tortoise pleaded.

"How did you say Hare plans to beat Antelope in the race," asked his mother-in-law.

"Err... I didn't say. I don't know... err... I have to go, please," replied Tortoise, standing up and heading towards the door.

"No, he didn't say," said his father-in-law. "I think what he said was that he was considering racing against Hare. Tortoise, isn't that what you said?"

"No... that wasn't what—"

"Oh, you said something about the new time", interjected the father-in-law.

"So what is the new time for the race?" asked his mother-in-law.

"Time?" asked Tortoise, "I didn't... I don't know... I really have to go now." Tortoise opened the door.

"Alright, then," said his father-in-law. "Thank you for coming.

"Are you sure you still don't want more yam pottage?" his mother-in-law asked.

"I'm sure. Thank you very much," Tortoise replied, his voice trembling as he dashed into the night.

As the door closed, Tortoise's parents-in-laws collapsed with the laughter they had been holding in all the while.

Moonlight reflected off the puddles on the road and shimmered off the leaves on the trees. Crickets chirped in perfect harmony into the well-lit night, but Tortoise didn't notice any of nature's beauty, as he ran home. He wiped his face as he went even faster, running into the puddles and almost crashing into the trees. The burning sensation on his head was all he could think of. He would have taken off his cap as soon as he left his parents-in-laws' house, but most of the animals were outside their homes enjoying the night breeze. Tortoise didn't want them to see him take off a pottage-filled cap from his head. As Tortoise sped by, some of the animals called out greetings, while others wanted to know why he was in such a hurry. But Tortoise didn't stop to respond. Never had his house seemed so distant.

At last, he sighted his home. But just as he was about to take off his cap, a voice called out to him.

"Tortoise, where have you been?" It was his neighbour, Dog. "We've been waiting for you for hours." Dog and a few other animals were sitting in front of Tortoise's house.

"What? What in the world for?" Tortoise snapped as he struggled to unlock his door.

"It's your turn to host the board games," said Pig. "Or have you forgotten?"

Tortoise didn't respond. He kept trying to get the door open.

"Are you okay?" asked Goat. "Why are you shaking so much? And what's that aroma? Smells like... yam pottage."

Still Tortoise said nothing as he continued to

battle with the door. Dog walked up to the door and turned the knob. "It's already open," he said to Tortoise.

Tortoise dashed inside, slammed the door and threw off his cap. Then he screamed. Dog and the others outside rushed inside to find Tortoise rubbing his scalp.

"I am bald," Tortoise yelled. "All my hair is gone! I am bald!"

The confused animals looked down at the cap with its contents of yam pottage mixed with hair, and then they looked at each other.

"I am bald," Tortoise screamed again. "The hot yam pottage has burnt off my hair!"

4

Why Chicken is served at Celebrations

It was the beginning of the planting season and the animals had been working on their farms every day from dawn. One day as they returned to their homes, tired and happy for the day's work, they talked about the planting season, their crops, and the coming festival. Just as they began to settle into their homes, Hawk, the king's messenger, picked up his gong, flapped his wings and began to fly from house to house.

"Gong! Gong! Gong!" Hawk struck his gong as he landed on the roof of the first house on his path. "All the animals must be at the Royal Palace at sunset for a very important meeting. Gong! Gong! Gong! All the animals in this kingdom must be at the Royal Palace by sundown for a very important meeting with Lion the king! Gong! Gong! Gong!"

Some of the animals had just enough time for a short nap and a light meal before they headed to the palace. They all wondered what the meeting was about.

"It must be about the fallen tree by the river bank," Fox said, nodding his head to Tiger.

"I don't think so," replied Tiger. "Ox and Elephant moved it out of the way this morning."

"Maybe it is about the upcoming festival," suggested Bird with excitement. "I can't wait!"

"It has to be really important to hold at the Royal Palace," said Tortoise.

"We will know soon enough," said Owl.

When Hawk got to Hen's house and repeated the

message, Hen said she already had an engagement for the evening. "You see," said Hen, "I am just heading to a party. The water animals invited me to their annual party, and I already promised I would be there."

"I see," said the Hawk. "But the other land animals who were also invited by the water animals just told me they would cancel their plans and come for the meeting at the palace instead. It is a very important meeting and King Lion is expecting all of us to be there."

"Hmm. I don't think I can miss this party," Hen said. "From what I have heard, the party is going to be something! You can't imagine the dishes that will be served there. And if indeed all the other land animals will no longer be attending, I will have a lot more to eat." Hen licked and smacked her lips.

Hawk shook his head, "Priorities, Hen. This meeting at the palace is a very important one. King Lion has summoned all of us."

"Don't make a fuss, Hawk. I will stop by your house on my way from the party to find out what was so important about the palace meeting."

Lion welcomed the animals to the meeting. "My

fellow animals," he said, "thank you for being here at such short notice. I have asked us to gather here to decide, once and for all, on a very important issue. As you know, during celebrations and festivals many dishes are served — sometimes, too many!" The king paused and all the animals nodded their heads in agreement. "Today," continued Lion, "we must decide on which of us, henceforth, will be served as the main dish during celebrations and festivals."

The animals began to whisper among themselves. "At least now we know why we are here," muttered Pig, "and it's about time we made that decision." The animals beside him nodded in agreement.

"So, any volunteers?" asked Lion, looking around at the animals.

"In the absence of volunteers," continued Lion after a while, "does any animal want to nominate another?"

When none of the animals responded to Lion's call, he asked each animal to give reasons why he or she should not be chosen as the main dish during celebrations and festivals.

"I am too bony," yelled Lizard quickly.

"Oh, I love bones," said Dog. "Lizard would be a good dish indeed."

"But most of us like to chew on something fleshy," interjected Hyena.

"I am beautiful," said Butterfly, "but there's nothing on me worth eating."

"If I am chosen, where will honey come from?" asked Bee.

"I can't imagine my honey-pot without a single drop of honey!" exclaimed Bear, smacking his lips.

"I have other responsibilities already," said Dog. "I have to work on the farm, lead the vigilante group, help when there is a fire and a whole lot more."

"How about Goat or Hen?" asked Pig.

"Why not you?" responded Goat sharply. "I have been told you're rather tasty."

"But not as juicy as you are," grunted Pig.

"That's enough!" said Lion. "Next!"

The animals took turns justifying why they should not be served as the primary celebration dish.

When it was Rabbit's turn to speak, his voice

only came out in a whisper. He had always found it difficult to speak boldly. He tried to speak again, but his voice still came out in a whisper.

"We can't hear you!" yelled the other animals.

Rabbit, feeling very embarrassed, tried to make himself invisible. He kept his head down and his eyes to the ground. "Don't chicken out now," said his friend, Monkey, "just speak up."

Rabbit took a deep breath, cleared his throat and spoke as loud as he could: "I don't think I will be so...yummy."

There was a pause as the animals looked him over. "True," one of them said finally, "Rabbit doesn't look like he would be delicious."

Next to speak was Sheep. He opened his mouth but no words came out. He knew exactly what he wanted to say, but he just couldn't get the words out. All the animals stared at him impatiently. The words floated in Sheep's head, but just wouldn't come out of his mouth. "What if the other animals laugh at my voice?" he thought. He whispered to Owl who was perched on a branch next to him, "What if they think what I say isn't sensible?"

"We are waiting," said Leopard.

"Just a minute," Owl replied as she smiled down at Sheep and said, "Remember, fortune favours the bold."

Owl's words were exactly what Sheep needed to hear. "Fortune favours the bold," he murmured to himself. Now with confidence, Sheep cleared his throat and said to the gathering, "I don't want to be the main celebration dish, because I don't want to be."

There was silence in the meeting as the animals stared at Sheep.

"That's good enough reason," said Lion, "Next!"

The animals looked around, but there was no other animal left to speak.

"We don't have all night," said Lion, "Next!" he repeated.

"We have all spoken," said Antelope.

"All, except Hen, who is not at this meeting," said Hawk.

"Where is she?" Lion asked with a frown. "Didn't she get the message?"

Hawk explained that Hen, like all the animals present had been told about the meeting. However,

Hen said she had made plans to attend the annual celebration of the water animals.

Lion stood up and cleared his throat. "Well, this makes it much easier than I had imagined. Since Hen is the only animal not present to give reasons why she shouldn't be the main celebration dish, we can all agree that she will in fact have to be."

All the animals agreed that this was the best decision. And this is why there is always chicken to feast on at celebrations and festivals.

5

The Broken Pot

Once, there was a poor widow who lived with her daughter in a tiny village. They didn't have much to eat or beautiful clothes to wear. The poor widow had a small farm where she grew food for them to eat and sell, and for extra income, she worked on other people's farms as well.

The widow was very hard working and always reminded her daughter to be diligent. Her daughter,

Ada, was a pleasant young girl. She was very polite and helpful to her mum, but was also very playful. If the widow asked Ada to bring in the clothes from the line outside at a certain time, Ada would forget, run off to play, and bring them in hours later. If she was asked to sweep the front yard, she would sweep only about half and then spend the rest of the time chasing butterflies. The widow often advised her daughter to spend her time wisely by playing only after she had completed her house chores and anything else she had been asked to do. "Do the right thing at the right time, Ada," she would say. "There is a time for everything."

One day, the poor widow asked Ada to go to the stream to fetch water. "Go directly to the stream and return home immediately," she said.

"May I go later?" Ada asked. "Let me just finish the game I'm playing with my friends outside, Mama, then I will go and fetch the water."

"When is later, Ada?" her mother asked. "Can't you see it will soon get dark? Ada, how many times do I have to tell you that there is a time for everything? Go and get the water. If it isn't dark when you return, then you can go out to play with your friends." The widow reached for the water pot from a top shelf. "Make sure you rinse the pot when you get to the stream. Be careful with this pot, Ada; it's been in the family for many, many years. My mother gave it to me on my wedding day, and she told me her own mother gave it to her at her own wedding."

"Yes, Mama," said Ada, "I know. You have told me many times." Ada was impatient to get going. She wanted to hurry so she could come back to play before dark. Ada swung the pot in the air and skipped towards the door.

"Be careful with the pot!" the widow said again to her daughter.

The widow looked forward to the day she would give the pot to Ada as part of her wedding gift. She wished she could store the pot away and never have to use it before that day. But she had only one other pot that was less valuable and which she used for cooking and other house chores. It was now very old and leaked in many parts. She was saving to buy another pot, but until then, she had no choice but to use her precious pot. She only hoped Ada would be very careful with it.

Ada hurried towards the stream. As she trudged along, she saw many children playing and wondered why her mother always had to send her on errands during the best play times of the evening. She passed some girls building and decorating sand houses, she saw some chasing after butterflies, and others dancing and singing. She desperately wanted to join them, but her mother's words kept playing in her head. All Ada could do was to rush as fast as she could to fetch the water before the other children went back to their homes. "I just can't wait to get back and join in the fun," she thought to herself as she ran.

At the stream, she saw more children swimming and splashing water on one another. Again, she was tempted to join them, but her mother's warning rang in her ears. Ada filled her pot quickly and headed home.

She walked as fast as the pot she had balanced on her head would let her. Just as she took the bend home, some of her friends saw her. "Hey, Ada, the *suwe* champion," one girl called out. "We've been waiting for you to join our team."

"No, Ada you have to join our team," said another girl.

"I will be back soon, let me just get this water home to my mother," Ada responded. She was now more in a hurry to get home.

"Ada please, please come. Just for one round and then you can go home, please..."

Ada stopped. She looked forward at her home, just ahead, and back at her friends just behind. "Should I, should I not?" she wondered. "Okay," she called out, "just for one round." Ada walked back to join her friends. She lifted the pot of water from her head and placed it gently under a tree.

Ada threw the stone, which landed perfectly within the drawn lines. She then hopped on the squares, skipping the one marked with the stone. The other girls cheered and applauded as Ada played flawlessly till she completed the course for all the squares.

The chants of "we won! Hey, we won," filled the air as the winning team danced in excitement.

Ada ran to pick up her pot. She balanced it on her head and began running home. As she ran, she turned to take one last wistful look at her friends who had started a game of "ten-ten". As she did, she stepped on a huge stone and lost her balance. Her mother's precious pot fell and shattered.

Ada burst into tears. She knew her mother would be disheartened. "I was almost home; why did I stop. Why didn't I take the pot of water straight home?" In tears, Ada began to sing:

Nne e Nne e	*Mother Mother*
Udu m araputa m'o o	*My pot has led me into trouble*
Udu!	*Pot!*
Nne e Nne e	*Mother Mother*
Udu m araputa m'o o	*My pot has led me into trouble*
Udu!	*Pot!*
Udu m ji chube iyi	*The pot I used to fetch from the stream*
Na mu amaghi n'udu awaa	*I didn't know when the pot got broken*
Udu!	*Pot!*
Udu m ji chube iyi	*The pot I used to fetch from the stream*
Na mu amaghi n'udu awaa	*I didn't know when the pot got broken*

The Broken Pot

Udu!	*Pot!*
Ụkwụ akpọọ m	*On missing my step*
O we bụrụ n'udu awaa	*That's how the pot got broken*
Udu!	*Pot!*
Ọ bụ kam soro udu?	*Should I go after the pot?*
Ka ọbụ mụ ghara udu naba?	*Or should I leave the pot and go home?*
Udu!	*Pot!*
Ọ bụ kam soro udu?	*Should I go after the pot?*
Ka ọbụ mụ ghara udu naba?	*Or should I leave the pot and go home?*
Udu!	*Pot!*
Udu Mama a	*Mama's Pot*
Udu!	*Pot!*
Udu Nne mo o	*My Mother Pot*
Udu!	*Pot!*
Ọ bụ m naba a?	*Should I keep going?*
Udu!	*Pot!*
I'sịm naba a?	*Do you say I should go?*
Udu!	*Pot!*

Ọ bụ m naba o?	*Should I keep going?*
Udu!	*Pot!*
I'sịm naba o?	*Do you say l should go?*
Udu!	*Pot!*
Ewo Nne mo o	*Ewo[2] my Mother o!*
Nne Nne mo o	*Mother my Mother o!*
Ewo Nne mo o	*Ewo, my Mother o!*
Nne Nne mo o	*Mother my Mother o!*
Agam atọ na akwa?	*Will I keep crying?*
Ewo o!	*Ewo o!*
Agam atọ n'akwa?	*Will I keep crying?*
Ewo o!	*Ewo o!*
Agam atọ n'akwa?	*Will I keep crying?*
Nne mo o o	*My Mother o o o!*

---

2 A cry of sorrow

6

Tortoise and the Drum

A long time ago there was severe famine in the animal kingdom. The rains had not fallen for many seasons and the animals were starving.

One day, while Tortoise was out foraging for food, he passed by a very tall palm tree that used to have luscious palm fruits. He sighed as he looked up at the grey and withered palm fronds and wondered how long the drought in the land would last. As he was about to look away, he saw, in the midst of the grey-brown decaying fronds, something red and shiny. On a closer look, Tortoise realised it was a palm fruit hidden and almost covered by the dying fronds.

Wasting no time, he climbed up the palm tree and plucked the fruit. He could not believe his luck. As he was about to toss the fruit into his mouth, it fell from his hand and rolled down towards a large hole in the ground. Tortoise clambered down the tree and went after the fruit. As he was about to pick it up, his fingers pushed against it and it fell into the hole. "No!" exclaimed Tortoise as he watched the palm fruit roll farther away.

Tortoise jumped into the hole in search of the fruit, but instead of finding the palm fruit, he came across another hole. He figured that the fruit must have rolled into the second hole. "I must find my fruit," Tortoise said to himself as he jumped into this hole. There was a long, narrow path in the second hole, which Tortoise took, until he got to the home of the underground animals.

"Stop! You are eating my palm fruit," Tortoise

yelled as he saw the underground animals nibbling on his palm fruit. The underground animals had just taken the last bite off the fruit. "Do you know how much work I put into getting that fruit from the tree?" he demanded, staring at them in anger. "Do you know when last I ate anything good?"

"Had we known the palm fruit belonged to you, we would not have eaten it," responded one of the underground animals.

"Well, how will you compensate me now?" Tortoise asked, looking around. "Do you have anything good here that I can eat?"

The animals shook their heads.

"We are deeply sorry for unknowingly depriving you of your palm fruit," said an elder of the underground animals. "Please, accept this drum as a peace offering."

"Drum? Drum?" Tortoise shrieked. "I am hungry and you offer me a drum! Will music take away my hunger?"

"Actually, it will," replied the elder.

"Don't you make a mockery of me!"

"This is not an ordinary drum," said the elder. "Whenever you are hungry, beat the drum seven times and it will bring you all the food you want."

It took a while for Tortoise to be convinced, but at last, after the elder gave a demonstration of what the drum could do, his anger was replaced by a smile.

"Thank you, thank you very much," Tortoise said. "You can have my palm fruit, I don't need it anymore."

"Make sure the drum is never touched by dirt," the elder called after Tortoise, who was excitedly climbing out the hole with the drum secure under his arm.

As soon as he stepped into his hut, Tortoise called his wife and children to tell them what had happened.

His wife was sceptical. "Beat the drum then," she said.

Tortoise beat the drum seven times and a feast appeared before them. They fell on the food with gusto. When the family had eaten as much as they could, there was still a lot of food left.

"Even the best harvest could not have provided the crops to cook these delicacies," Tortoise's wife said.

Tortoise dug a hole in a corner of their hut, wrapped up the drum and hid it in the ground. Then Tortoise went out and gathered all the animals to his hut.

"I don't know why and I don't know how, but somehow I have been bestowed with the power to provide food for all of you," he said to them.

"Here we go again with Tortoise and one of his tricks," said Owl, rolling her eyes.

"We are too hungry to be pranked, Tortoise, if this is one of your…" Tiger stopped mid-sentence when he saw Tortoise's wife and children presenting different dishes to the animals.

Never had the animals seen so much food, not even during any of their festivals. They grabbed this food and that food, most of them eating with both hands at the same time.

"Tortoise, you have saved our lives," they said. "Thank you very much."

For days, Tortoise fed the entire kingdom. All the animals talked about was how they were only alive because of Tortoise's ability to provide food. As the animals ate and praised him, Tortoise swelled with pride, and soon he began to imagine himself not only as the saviour of the animal kingdom, but also as the king. He knew that, so long as he kept feeding the kingdom, it would only be a matter of time before the animals would crown him king. Already, some animals had begun to seek his counsel on issues, while others were offering to serve him.

But Lion was the king of the animal kingdom, and he was beginning to feel threatened by Tortoise's growing popularity. "The more the animals depend on Tortoise, the less they would need me or see me as their king," Lion said to himself. "Tortoise and his cunning ways... perhaps this is a trick to steal my throne."

Lion decided to find the source of Tortoise's food and take it for himself.

One day, while Tortoise was out visiting, Lion went to his home. Tortoise's wife welcomed Lion and told him that Tortoise was not home. "I am aware of that," said Lion. "But I spoke to him. We agreed that, for safety, you should hand over the source of his food to me so it is kept in my palace."

Tortoise's wife was surprised that her husband would make such a decision without discussing with her, and that he didn't come himself to give

Lion the drum. "Your highness, why don't we bring it to you tomorrow morning?" she said.

"And if it is stolen tonight, how would the kingdom survive?" Lion snapped. "Bring me your husband's source of food at once!"

Tortoise's wife walked slowly to a corner of their hut, dug out the drum and gave it to Lion. Lion took the drum and ran to his palace, raising dust and kicking mud as he went.

King Lion sent the town crier to summon all the animals to his palace that evening. "Tell them that, henceforth, the feast will hold in my palace, as the power of providing food for the kingdom has now been conferred on me, their king."

Tortoise was furious when he learned that Lion had taken the drum. When he went to Lion's palace to ask for his drum, the palace guards would not let him in. Tortoise returned home distraught.

That evening, all the animals gathered expectantly at the palace for their feast. "This feast will be even greater than the others since it is a royal feast," the animals said.

With the drum in his hands, Lion welcomed all the animals. He beat the drum once, but nothing happened. He beat the drum a second time, still there was no food. He beat the drum again and again until at the seventh time, the palace was suddenly filled with food.

But this food was different. It was rotten and smelly! Holding their breaths and covering their mouths, the animals ran out of the palace to escape the stench.

Lion had never felt so humiliated. "I should never have seized the drum from its rightful owner," he said to himself. "I must apologise to Tortoise and the entire kingdom."

When the animals told Tortoise what had happened at the palace, Tortoise was very happy. He knew Lion must have got the drum dirty.

"Am I not the saviour of the animal kingdom?" Tortoise said to the animals. "Return to your homes and I will have food for all of you in the morning." Tortoise knew this was his opportunity to become king. He would go back to get another drum from the underground animals, but this time, he would not feed any of the animals unless they crowned him king.

Tortoise took a groundnut and headed to the

home of the underground animals. He threw the groundnut into the hole and, after waiting for a while, jumped into the hole and then down the second hole through the long, narrow path until he got to the home of the underground animals.

"Stop!" you are eating my groundnut,"Tortoise yelled, running towards the underground animals he saw nibbling on his groundnut. Tortoise moved closer to make sure the animals had taken the last bite off the groundnut.

"Do you know how much work I put into getting

that nut from the ground?" he demanded, looking furious. "Groundnuts are rare in my kingdom these days and the drum you gave me has never served them."

"Had we known the groundnut belonged to you, we would not have eaten it," responded one of the underground animals.

"Well, how will you compensate me?" Tortoise asked. "Do you have another magical drum for me?"

"We are deeply sorry for unknowingly depriving you of your groundnut," said an elder of the underground animals. "Please, accept this second magical drum as a peace offering."

"Thank you, thank you," Tortoise said with a knowing smile. "You can have my groundnut, I don't need it anymore."

With the drum securely under his arm, Tortoise ran all the way home.

In the morning, all the animals gathered outside Tortoise's home. Lion was there too. He called for attention, confessed his wrong and apologised to all the animals. He also apologised to Tortoise and his wife.

When Lion finished speaking, Tortoise cleared

his throat and said, "We have heard what our king has to say, but you will agree with me that the animal who saves the kingdom should be king."

Some animals nodded while others shook their heads at the prospect of Tortoise as their king.

"Well, I will only serve you food if you make me your king," he declared.

The animals began to deliberate and argue among themselves.

"Wouldn't that be disloyal to Lion?" said some animals.

"But Tortoise is right; the saviour of the kingdom should be the king of the kingdom," said other animals.

Maybe seeing the feast will help convince them, Tortoise thought as he began to beat the drum. When Tortoise beat the drum the seventh time, a buzzing sound began to come out of it. As the animals watched, a swarm of bees flew out of the drum and began to chase Tortoise. Tortoise ran, and the bees chased him far, far away from the kingdom.

7

Why Monkeys Live
in the Forest

Monkey has always lived in the forest. Every day, he would swing from tree to tree to its edge so that he could spy on the humans in the nearby village. Monkey would then return to his home, sit beside a puddle or hang from a tree over the stream and admire his features. He was very curious and also very vain.

"I am one of few animals that can boast of some resemblance to the humans," Monkey would say proudly to himself. Then as he thought more about the humans, Monkey's proud smile would gradually fade into a frown. "Oh, how I wish I could be exactly like them," he would say with a sigh, "without hair all over my body, and without a tail."

The more Monkey observed the humans and compared himself to them, the more he wanted to become human. He wanted to walk upright and talk like them. He wanted to sing and dance and live in a house and wear clothes.

Soon Monkey could think of nothing else. Many nights, he would lay awake imagining life as a human being: what his voice would sound like, how gracefully he would walk and how silky his skin would be.

One day, Monkey made up his mind to find a way to be human, so he went to the Creator for help.

"I would like to live in the human village," he said.

"Why? Your home is here in the forest, Monkey,"

the Creator replied. "Is there something about your home that does not please you?"

Monkey told the Creator how much he admired the humans and wanted to live among them, doing the things they did.

"You can only live in the village if you are human," said the Creator. "Are you actually asking to become human?"

Monkey nodded slowly.

"Monkey, you know that when I created you, I made you perfect," the Creator said gently.

"I have given my decision a lot of thought," Monkey responded. "Being human will make me more perfect!"

"Very well, then," said the Creator. "I will do as you have asked, on one condition. Humans are far more than what you see on the outside. There are certain attributes good humans must possess and you must be tested on at least one of them before you can become human. You will be tested on self-discipline."

The Creator told Monkey that to pass the test, he must stay in his section of the forest for seven consecutive days without going anywhere. If

Monkey passed the test, the Creator promised to transform him to a human on the seventh day.

Monkey was very happy. "This is such an easy task," he said to himself. "I can't wait to step out of this forest as a human being in seven days."

The first day came and went.

The second day came and went.

The third day came and went.

The fourth day came and went.

By the fifth day, Monkey became anxious. The days seemed longer than usual. "Just two more days, just two more days," he kept repeating to himself.

On the sixth day, Monkey woke to the sound of music and merrymaking. The humans were having a ceremony. The music seemed to come from every part of the forest. "It must be an important festival," Monkey said to himself. "I wonder how they are dancing and what they are wearing." He climbed the tallest tree, but he could not see into the village from his part of the forest.

The tempo of the music quickened and the monkey began to move his head in tune. As the drums reverberated through the forest, Monkey climbed down the tree and began dancing. "This time tomorrow, I will be out there with them," he said, laughing. As Monkey danced, he began to sing in tune with the music.

Ma d' èniyàn	*I'll become human*
ma d' èniyàn	*I'll become human*
Ní 'wòyí ọla	*By this time tomorrow*
ma d' èniyàn	*I'll become human*
Ma d' èniyàn	*I'll become human*
ma d' èniyàn	*I'll become human*
Ní 'wòyí ọla	*By this time tomorrow*
ma d' èniyàn	*I'll become human*
Irun t'ówà lára mi yi kò ní sí mọ́ o	*I'll no longer have hairy skin*
Ma d'èniyàn	*I'll become human*
ma d' èniyàn	*I'll become human*
Ìrù t'ówà ni'di mi yi kò ní sí mọ́ o	*I'll no longer have a tail*
Ma d' èniyàn	*I'll become human*
ma d'èniyàn	*I'll become human*

Ma k'ẹ̀sẹ̀ méjì s'ílẹ̀, ma rin, ma yan	*I'll stand on two feet and walk majestically*
Ma d'ènìyàn	*I'll become human*
ma d'ènìyàn	*I'll become human*

Monkey was so caught up in the bliss of the moment that he didn't realise that he was dancing towards the human village. Tree after tree, Monkey swung and sang away, till he got to the edge of the forest and then into human village.

The villagers were surprised to see a monkey singing and dancing towards them. They had never seen anything like it. The music slowly died down and finally stopped as the humans watched the dancing monkey and listened to his song.

Slowly, Monkey became aware of the humans staring at him. He went quiet at once.

"How is it possible that you will be human tomorrow?" they asked.

"The Creator promised to make me human if I passed the self-discipline test by staying in my section of the forest for seven consecutive days. Tomorrow will be the seventh day!"

The humans exchanged confused glances. "So you are to stay in your section of the forest for seven consecutive days, after which the Creator will make you human?" they asked.

"Exactly!" Monkey answered happily. "As long as I don't leave my home before tomorrow, I – "

Only then did it dawn on Monkey that he had in fact left his home on the sixth day. He turned and ran back towards the forest, swinging from tree to tree until he arrived at his home.

The Creator was waiting for him. You failed the test, Monkey," the Creator said. "So, I am sorry, you will never become human or live in the village. You will remain as I have created you and live in the forest."

8

Three Unwise Men

One day, three young men went into the forest to pluck some *dinya*. The fruit had just come into season and the men were eager to eat some.

"I was so glad when the rains finally stopped," said one of the men. "*Dinya* wouldn't have ripened with all that rain. Now, I am going to eat as many as my stomach can hold and then take home as many as my hands can hold."

"Hands? I brought this basket so I can put all the *dinya* I can in it!" said the second young man.

"Basket? I plan to take back the seeds and plant *dinya* trees all around my hut!" said the third man.

After a long walk, they came across a cluster of *dinya* trees. The young men climbed up one of the trees and began to feast on *dinya*. They were still up on the tree eating the fruits when they heard sounds of galloping horses coming towards them. When the young men recognised the horsemen as slave raiders, they became terrified.

"I don't want to be taken captive," said one of the men, "we must split up and hide. I will hide on the tree. The leaves will keep them from spotting me."

The second man climbed down and hid behind an anthill. "They won't see me if I crouch here and stay very still."

The third man chose to hide in the tall grass. "This grass is thick enough to keep me hidden," he said.

As the horsemen rode closer, the ground began to tremble and the trees shook. The ripe *dinya* began to drop off the trees.

The man hiding in the tall grass jumped out into the open and waved to the men as they rode past. "Do ride gently so you don't cause all the *dinya* to fall at once," he called out.

"Ah! This one will make a prudent slave," said the slave raiders, and the man was captured.

The man hiding behind the anthill saw his friend being captured and shouted to the raiders, "Let my friend go!"

"Ah! This one will make a loyal slave," said the slave raiders, and the man was also captured.

"These men are indeed unwise," laughed the slave raiders. "We would not have seen them at all if they hadn't come out of hiding. Maybe they ate something that affected their judgment."

"You are mistaken," shouted the third man from up the tree. The only thing they have eaten today is *dinya* and it doesn't cause bad judgment!"

"Ah! This one will make a dutiful slave," the slave raiders said. The third man was captured, and the slave raiders rode away with all three men.

9

The Talking Tree

Many years ago, in a distant village far up the
northern hills, there lived a boy named Audu.
Audu loved to play pranks on people. He loved
to hide in the bush and startle people when they
went by. Sometimes while he played with his
friends, he would start screaming, "Snake! Snake!"
or "Scorpion! Big scorpion!" and everyone would

run away in fright, while he would reel around in laughter.

Audu didn't play pranks only on his peers. Sometimes he played the pranks on adults and even on his parents at home. He would scream for fire when there was no fire. He would scream out in pain when he was not hurt, and when he'd get all the attention, he would laugh and laugh till tears rolled down his face.

His parents had warned him about this habit; many of the adults had told him to be careful or one day he would call for help and no one would answer because they would think it was another of his pranks. Everyone told him that his pranks could get someone hurt or get him in trouble, but Audu did not listen.

One harmattan evening, Audu was walking leisurely down a bush path, chewing on a date palm when he noticed a tree with a big hole in its trunk. He stepped closer to inspect the tree and found that the trunk was hollow. It was a very big baobab tree and the hollow, as Audu found, was as big as a house. Audu became excited. "This would make a good hiding place," he said as he climbed in through the hole. He was looking around inside the tree, happy at his find, when he heard footsteps coming from the bush path. Audu immediately had one of his prank ideas.

The footsteps belonged to a woman who seemed to be coming from the market with her basket of fruits. When she was close enough, Audu bellowed out from the tree:

"*Trader! Trader with the basket of fruits, come here!*"

The woman was so startled that the basket she balanced on her head almost fell off. She stopped and looked around her to see who had called, but there was no one behind her or in the bushes beside her.

"*Trader with the basket of fruits, it is I, the tree, beckoning on you.*"

"The tree is talking? That tree is talking!" yelled the woman as she dropped her basket of fruits and fled.

A young farmer was next.

"*Farmer! Farmer with the hoe and cutlass, come here!*"

The young farmer was so startled that the hoe he balanced on his shoulder almost fell off. He stopped and looked around him to see who had called, but there was no one behind him or in the bushes beside him.

"*Farmer with the hoe and cutlass, it is I, the tree, beckoning on you.*"

"The tree is talking? That tree is talking!" yelled the young farmer as he dropped his hoe and cutlass and fled.

A hunter was next.

"*Hunter with the animal hide, come here!*"

The hunter was so startled that the hide he balanced on his head almost fell off. He stopped and looked around him to see who had called, but there was no one behind him or in the bushes beside him.

"*Hunter with the animal hide, it is I, the tree, beckoning on you.*"

"The tree is talking? That tree is talking!" yelled the hunter as he dropped the animal hide and fled.

A milkmaid was next.

"*Milkmaid with the calabash, come here!*"

The milkmaid was so startled that the calabash she had balanced on her head almost fell off. She stopped and looked around her to see who had called, but there was no one behind her or in the bushes beside her.

"*Milkmaid with the calabash, it is I, the tree, beckoning on you.*"

"The tree is talking? That tree is talking!" yelled the milkmaid as she dropped her calabash and fled.

Each time, Audu had a good laugh as the people fled in fright.

The people gathered in the distance and whispered about the mysterious talking tree. No one dared get close.

"You are a strong man," said one woman to a well-built man. "Surely, you can find out what the tree wants."

"This has nothing to do with physical strength," the man replied. "Something very evil has come to our village. I suggest we go home and shut ourselves in."

When Audu was sure no one was in sight, he climbed out of the tree, laughing. He picked up some of the fruits the trader had dropped on the ground and went home.

The mysterious talking tree became the terror of the village. Everyone was talking about it.

"That tree is very powerful," someone said. "Do you know it called my neighbour by name?"

"When the talking tree beckoned on me, I ran faster than a horse," another person said.

"Do you know it can see as far as the next village?" someone else said.

Whenever Audu heard people talking in hushed tones about the mysterious talking tree, he would secretly laugh and laugh. "That prank is my best yet; I must do it again, soon."

And soon enough Audu was back in the tree, calling out to people as they walked by. This time, he made the tree scarier. From inside the trunk he growled and made strange noises. He told a little girl he would eat her, and that he would swallow up the whole village. Every day, Audu stole in and out of the tree and frightened people so much that they could no longer go about their daily activities.

One day, the villagers could take it no more. They huddled together to discuss what they would do about the tree.

"This tree can't make us live in fear," said the farmer.

"We must do something about it before it swallows us up and wipes out our village," said the milkmaid.

"Let's cut the tree down," suggested the hunter.

"Yes, let's burn it up," another man added.

Chants of "Cut the tree!" "Burn it up!" "Cut the tree!" "Burn it up!" echoed through the village.

Audu was inside the tree when the people, bearing machetes and fire, surrounded it. Audu couldn't climb out without being seen. He knew he was in trouble.

When the first flame was thrown at the foot of the tree, Audu cried out. "Wait! Please, don't hurt me."

But the people did not stop. They wanted the tree to stop talking. They threw more fire at the tree, and soon it was smoking, with flames leaping all around it.

Audu kept screaming and crying and pleading with the people. "Please, stop! Please, stop! It is me, Audu. It's been me all long. Please, stop." He was waving his arms from the tree hollow but the people couldn't see him through the smoke.

At last, through the crackling fire, Audu's mother recognised the voice as Audu's at the instant everyone heard the voice crying, "It is me, Audu; it's been me all along. Please stop."

The people paused and listened, and sure enough, the voice from the tree was that of a boy. As they looked closer, they could see his little arms waving from the hollow in the tree.

Audu's mother began to wail. The women sobbed along with her and the men rushed to douse out the flames around the tree so they could get him out.

When Audu was finally pulled out of the tree, he had inhaled too much smoke and was unconscious.

After a while, Audu woke up and began to cry and plead with the people to forgive him. But the people were angry.

"So it was all a prank?"

"All these days, you were the voice in that tree scaring everyone and forcing us to remain indoors?"

"And this is not your first offence. You've been warned about your behaviour many times."

"Audu! How could you do this to our village?" his father scolded, reaching to hold up his sobbing wife.

The villagers were very angry and disappointed in Audu. Some of them even blamed his parents for not being able to stop him from playing pranks.

They decided that Audu must leave the village and never return.

"He will not do it again," sobbed his mother, "he is only a boy. He has learned his lesson."

"How can we protect ourselves from danger when we can't tell if it's truly danger or another prank from Audu?" the villagers asked. "Your entire family must leave the village."

Audu pleaded, and apologised; his parents pleaded along with him. But the villagers had had enough of Audu and his pranks.

And so Audu and his parents were banished from the village.

10

Why Tortoise has a Small Nose

Tortoise and Squirrel were very good friends. They shared their secrets and always helped each other when they had problems. When Tortoise was ill the previous month, it was Squirrel who bought the herbs for his friend's treatment. When a coconut fell on Squirrel's head, two weeks before, it was Tortoise who bought the balm to soothe his friend's pain.

The friends were both traders and had stalls in the biggest market in the region. Most mornings, they walked together to and from the market, discussing their plans for the day or their sales of the day.

One morning they arrived later than usual to the market and met the market already in full swing. Buyers moved from section to section and from stall to stall bargaining on items, while traders called out to customers and tried to convince them that their goods were the best in quality and price.

"Bananas for sale, bananas for sale!" shouted Monkey.

"Buy a dozen apples and get two free!" Giraffe called out.

"Stay healthy, eat fresh vegetables!" shouted Goat.

"Dry palm fronds for your roofs here!" Eagle sang over and over again.

"Wood for your fire!" Elephant called out.

The two friends quickly settled into their different stalls and began business for the day.

A while later, as Tortoise was showing Hen the delicate carvings on the plates he had for sale, shouts broke through the noise of trading.

"Let go of him. You both, stop fighting!" some voices shouted. The fighting seemed to be nearby. "I wonder which animals have got into a fight over customers this time?" said Hen, looking in the direction of the noise.

"Ignore them," said Tortoise, "let's talk business. As I was saying, it took days to —"

"Squirrel, let go of him!" a voice from the crowd yelled.

"Squirrel?" Tortoise paused. "Is my friend Squirrel the one fighting?" He asked Hen to excuse him for a moment, and he dashed out of his stall. Just by the vegetable stall, Tortoise saw Squirrel in a brawl with Mongoose.

"That's it, Squirrel," Tortoise cheered, "get him!"

But it seemed Mongoose was stronger, for as the crowd watched, Mongoose lifted Squirrel and threw him on the ground. It was at that moment that Tortoise jumped into the fight and began to punch Mongoose.

"Let go of me, Tortoise," Mongoose squeaked, "this has nothing to do with you."

"Tortoise, that's not fair! Leave him alone," a voice called from the crowd.

But Tortoise wouldn't listen. The other animals tried to pull him away. "You don't even know what started the fight, Tortoise," said Cheetah.

"I don't have to know to take sides with my friend!" Tortoise responded. By now he was holding Mongoose by the throat.

"Help!" whimpered Mongoose

More animals joined in to pull Tortoise away. But Tortoise held on.

"Let go of me, please," begged Mongoose. But Tortoise wouldn't budge. The animals tried to pry Mongoose away, but they only succeeded in loosening Tortoise's grip on his throat. In desperation, Mongoose opened his mouth, took Tortoise's nose between his teeth and bit hard.

"My nose," yelled Tortoise as his arms fell to his side. "My nose! Mongoose, my nose!" But Mongoose didn't let go.

In pain, Tortoise began to sing for help:

Asín t'òhun t'òkéré	*Mongoose and Squirrel*
jomìjo	*jomìjo*[3]
Àwọn ní wón jó n jà	*Were fighting each other*
jomìjo	*jomìjo*
Ìjà ré mo wá là	*I came to stop their fight*
jomìjo	*jomìjo*
Asín bá bù mí n'ímú jẹ	*Then Mongoose bit my nose*
jomìjo	*jomìjo*
Egbà mí lọ́wọ́ rẹ̀	*Please save me from him*
jomìjo	*jomìjo*
Àwò mí n bẹ lọ́jà	*My plates are still in the market*
jomìjooooo	*jomìjooooo*

Squirrel tried to pull Mongoose away, but the more he pulled, the harder Mongoose bit on Tortoise's nose.

The other animals did not immediately help Tortoise as he had not heeded their advice not to join the fight.

---

3 Onomatopoeic refrain

"Now you are on the receiving end, Tortoise," said Pig. "We asked you not to get involved; we asked you to let go of Mongoose, but you didn't listen."

Tortoise kept singing and looking to the animals for help.

"Please, Mongoose," Squirrel cried. "Let go of my friend. I am sorry; I should have accepted your apology for stepping on my toes, instead of hitting you."

"You should have come to make peace between Squirrel and Mongoose, instead of getting in the fight," said Jaguar to Tortoise.

When the animals thought Tortoise had been punished enough, they pleaded with Mongoose to let go of his nose. By the time Mongoose finally let go of Tortoise's nose, he had already bitten off a huge chunk.

11

The Race

Antelope always bragged that he was the fastest runner in the animal kingdom. He bragged so much that, one day, Frog decided to challenge him to a race.

"You? Race me?" Antelope laughed. "That would be an absolute waste of my time. You are clearly no match for me."

"That can only be proven after a race," Frog said. "You have to promise that if you lose, you will never brag again."

"Lose to you? Never! We will have this race tomorrow morning."

Frog knew he was indeed no match for Antelope. But he wanted to teach him a lesson in humility. He decided to enlist the help of his identical brothers to win the race.

Early the next morning, Frog positioned his brothers at different points along the course for the race.

"You will start the race," Frog said to one of his brothers.

"You will hide behind this bush," he said to another.

"You will hide behind this overgrown grass."

"You will hide behind this shrub."

"You will hide behind this tree."

"And I will hide here and finish the race."

Frog warned his brothers not to speak throughout the race. "No matter what Antelope says, do not utter a word," he said.

Antelope arrived at the starting line. He eyed

Frog and said, with a sneer, "I really should let you have a head start."

Frog kept his face to the ground and said nothing.

"You really think you can win this race?" Antelope asked. "Very well, then. Let the race begin."

Antelope and Frog charged forward and, in a flash, Antelope was way ahead of Frog.

Antelope ran along, thinking how easy the race would be to win. But just then, he saw Frog leaping in front of him. Antelope was surprised and impressed. He picked up his pace and quickly left Frog far behind.

Just as Antelope was starting to get comfortable again, he saw Frog ahead of him. Again, Antelope ran faster and overtook Frog. "Frog might be faster than I thought," said Antelope to himself, "but he is no match for me."

But soon, Antelope, to his surprise, saw Frog ahead of him yet again.

On and on they ran. One moment Antelope would run past Frog, and the next moment he would find Frog in front of him again.

Antelope was a few feet from the finish line

when he looked ahead and, to his utter shock, saw Frog leap across the finish line before him.

"I won! I won! I won!" Frog yelled.

Antelope returned to his home, humiliated and confused. "I know Frog is no match for me, so how did he win?" He asked himself over and over again.

Later that evening, Frog went to visit Antelope.

"Well, I won the race," Frog said to Antelope. "But I only won because I cheated. And I have come to apologise."

Frog told Antelope how his brothers had helped him. "I jumped out last from behind an anthill and completed the race," Frog said. "I did it because we were all tired of hearing you brag all the time. But I am sorry for cheating."

Antelope looked up gently at him and sighed. "I forgive you, Frog, and I thank you for teaching me a much needed lesson in humility."

12

Monkey and the Couple's Child

A long time ago, when humans and animals still lived amicably as neighbours, a farmer's wife gave birth to their first child after many, many years of longing for one. The couple, as expected, doted on the baby. The farmer and his wife used to work together on the farm daily, but after the baby was born, the farmer began to go alone while his wife stayed back at home to take care of their child. The farmer looked forward to returning home in the evenings to enjoy the company of his wife and baby.

As the weeks rolled by into harvest season, the farmer said to his wife, "I will need an extra hand on the farm if we are to harvest the crops in good time. But who will take care of our baby while we both work on the farm?"

The farmer's wife knew she had to help her husband; there was no way they could find someone to hire on the farm as everyone else was busy harvesting their own crops.

"I already thought about that," said the wife, "I think we should hire Monkey as nanny."

"Monkey? Are you sure?"

"Oh, yes. Monkey is experienced in caring for children; he helped our neighbours take care of their baby last year during the harvest. I hear he has helped other families care for their babies too."

The next morning, the wife took the baby to the farm with her husband. Before they began to work, she placed the baby under a tree and sang the song her neighbour had taught her to call out to Monkey:

Etok ebok	*Young Monkey*
Iya krong krong krong	*Iya krong krong krong*[4]
Etok ebok	*Young Monkey*
Iya krong krong krong	*Iya krong krong krong*
Iwang emedi	*The farm is open*
Iya krong krong krong	*Iya krong krong krong*
Di ben eyen	*Come for the child*
Iya krong krong krong	*Iya krong krong krong*
Etok ebok	*Young Monkey*
Iya krong krong krong	*Iya krong krong krong*
Etok ebok	*Young Monkey*
Iya krong krong krong	*Iya krong krong krong*

When Monkey heard the song, he came through the trees and took the baby away to care for him. The couple worked hard on their farm, harvesting

---

4 Onomatopoeic refrain

their corn, cassava and yams. When they were done for the day, the wife sang out to Monkey again:

Etok ebok	*Young Monkey*
Iya krong krong krong	*Iya krong krong krong*
Iwang eya eyong	*The farm is closed*
Iya krong krong krong	*Iya krong krong krong*
Ben eyen di	*Bring back the child*
Iya krong krong krong	*Iya krong krong krong*
Etok ebok	*Young Monkey*
Iya krong krong krong	*Iya krong krong krong*

When Monkey heard the song, he brought the baby back to his parents.

Every day, until the end of harvest, while farmer and wife worked on their farm, Monkey cared for the baby.

The next planting season, there was no rain, so all the crops withered. As the drought persisted, the food that families had stored in their homes depleted until nothing was left. People began to walk long distances in search of food.

One day, the farmer went again to dig all around his farm to see if he would find any tubers to take home to his wife and child. Not finding any, he sat on the ground in frustration, and as he ran his hands through the dry and thirsty earth, he wondered how they were going to survive. When he lifted his head, he saw Monkey sitting on a tree branch. And the farmer had an idea.

He returned home and told his wife of his idea and plan.

"Tomorrow," he said, "we will go to the farm and you will sing for Monkey to come out for the baby. After a while, you will sing for him to bring the baby back. When he returns the baby to you, I will hunt him down and we can cook him and eat him for weeks."

But the farmer's wife was not happy about the plan.

"If we eat Monkey, who will help us care for the child when the rains come and we have to plant?" she asked.

"The baby is fast growing. By the time the rains come, he will be able to sit in a corner on the farm while we work. For now, we need to make sure our baby does not starve."

Desperate for her beloved child's survival, the farmer's wife reluctantly agreed to the plan.

In the morning, the family went to their farm and the wife sang out to Monkey:

Etok ebok	*Young Monkey*
Iya krong krong krong	*Iya krong krong krong*
Etok ebok	*Young Monkey*
Iya krong krong krong	*Iya krong krong krong*
Iwang emedi	*The farm is open*
Iya krong krong krong	*Iya krong krong krong*
Di ben eyen	*Come for the child*
Iya krong krong krong	*Iya krong krong krong*
Etok ebok	*Young Monkey*
Iya krong krong krong	*Iya krong krong krong*
Etok ebok	*Young Monkey*
Iya krong krong krong	*Iya krong krong krong*

As usual, when Monkey heard the song, he came and took the baby away to help care for him. After some hours, the farmer's wife sang out to Monkey:

Etok ebok	*Young Monkey*
Iya krong krong krong	*Iya krong krong krong*
Iwang eya eyong	*The farm is closed*
Iya krong krong krong	*Iya krong krong krong*
Ben eyen di	*Bring back the child*
Iya krong krong krong	*Iya krong krong krong*
Etok ebok	*Young Monkey*
Iya krong krong krong	*Iya krong krong krong*

The farmer and his wife waited, but Monkey did not come back with their child.

The farmer's wife sang again, louder. Still, Monkey did not come out with their child.

The farmer and his wife became worried and wondered what could have gone wrong. The farmer's wife sang at the top of her voice for the third time. At last, from somewhere they could not tell, the couple heard Monkey begin to sing in response:

Ndieke	*I am not coming*
Iya krong krong krong	*Iya krong krong krong*
Ubet ke Ikot	*Your husband is in the bush*
Iya krong krong krong	*Iya krong krong krong*
Ikang ke Ubok	*With a rifle in his hand*
Iya krong krong krong	*Iya krong krong krong*
Aya ntop	*He will hunt me down*
Iya krong krong krong	*Iya krong krong krong*
Etok ebok	*Young Monkey*
Iya krong krong krong	*Iya krong krong krong*
Etok ebok	*Young Monkey*
Iya krong krong krong	*Iya krong krong krong*

The farmer and his wife were shocked. They wondered how Monkey had found out about their plan. They didn't know that Monkey, from the top of a tree, had seen the farmer hiding in the bush with his rifle.

Crying, the farmer's wife sang over and over again, pleading with Monkey to bring back their child. Each time she sang, Monkey responded with his own song.

Monkey never returned the child.

13

Why Pigs Sniff the Ground

Pig and Tortoise had been friends since they were young. They were often seen together playing in the market square, while their parents carried on with trading. They both loved folktales, and many evenings they would sit side by side in the village square looking into the face of the storytellers as they told one folktale after another. They shared the same interests and did everything together. Such was their closeness that despite the obvious differences in their physical features, many thought they were brothers.

This friendship continued into their adulthood. Pig and Tortoise even chose the same trade, becoming merchants like their parents. They both got married and had young ones. Pig's wife and Tortoise's wife became good friends, and their young played together just as their fathers had done. Business was profitable for the two friends; however, while Pig was prudent with his money, Tortoise spent his lavishly. Tortoise bought the latest of everything, even things he could not quite afford. He made sure other animals saw him giving to the poor. He liked when the animals talked about his generosity and about the things he owned. Tortoise enjoyed being the talk of the town. When he funded community projects like the roofing of the market stalls and the drainage by the stream, he bragged to the other animals about how his good deeds made their lives better.

Pig often cautioned Tortoise to be wise about his spending and save for a rainy day, but Tortoise never heeded Pig's advice. It seemed the more Pig told him to be discreet with his money, the more Tortoise spent.

Tortoise arrived at the market one day to find construction workers busy hammering, and laying bricks all around Gorilla's store. Gorilla was standing aside giving instructions to the workers. Tortoise went over to him.

"What's going on?" asked Tortoise. "What's with all the noise?

"Good morning, Tortoise," said Gorilla. "I am just expanding my store. I have been saving for two years for this. Two long years. I am just glad that I can now afford to grow my business," Gorilla added with a smile.

Tortoise smiled back at him. "Ah, very nice. It's exactly what I had in mind too," Tortoise said, "though I have planned on not only expanding to the back, but also to the front and to the sides. In fact, I need to hurry there; the builders should be arriving any time now." Tortoise had been speaking loudly so the animals close by could hear.

When Tortoise arrived at his store, he looked at it and wondered where he would get the money for any expansion. "I just have to figure out how to expand my store because it has to be the largest in this market," he thought. Instead of opening up for the day's business, Tortoise went home to think about how he could get the money to enlarge his store.

Tortoise did not go to the market the rest of the week because he did not want the other animals to ask why the construction work had not started on his store. Pig visited him on his way from the market to know if anything was wrong, but Tortoise said he just wasn't feeling well. A few days later, Pig visited again, and during their conversation, he said to Tortoise, "All the animals in the market have been talking about how huge your store will be when all the expansion has been completed."

Tortoise nodded in response.

"What do you need all that space for?" asked Pig.

Tortoise knew his friend did not support his extravagant spending, so he said, "I just bought a lot of goods and I need more space to store them." He sighed and shook his head, "In fact, the reason I haven't been feeling well is that I don't have enough money to expand, and the goods will be delivered very soon."

Pig felt sorry for Tortoise, but he said nothing, only shook his head.

"This is a very profitable business," continued Tortoise. "I was actually wondering if you would loan me the money for the building. Once the goods have been sold, I will repay you with interest."

Pig told Tortoise to allow him sleep over his proposal. The next morning, just as Cock crowed, Tortoise knocked on Pig's door. "Have you made a decision yet?" he asked Pig anxiously. "I tell you, my friend, you will not regret this investment. I will return your money in exactly three months."

Pig sighed and said to Tortoise, "A friend in need is a friend indeed, so I will give you the loan. Please note, however, that it is the money I have been putting aside to build a new home for my family, and with new piglets on the way, I must have the house ready in six months."

Tortoise thanked Pig and told him he would have more than enough to build a new home because of the interest on the loan.

In the coming weeks, Tortoise was seen supervising the construction work on his store, giving loud instructions to the builders for all the animals to hear. Whenever another animal commented on the progress of the work, Tortoise would respond loudly, "Oh thank you - My store is going to be the largest in the market, for sure."

Soon, the work was done and Tortoise's store became, indeed, the largest in the market. All the animals talked about its imposing size. Tortoise wouldn't have had it any other way. He walked around the market with a spring in his steps and his head up, smiling as the animals whispered about his grand store whenever they saw him pass by.

After three months, Pig asked Tortoise for his money. "Please give me one more month," said Tortoise, "I will surely refund your money."

Pig waited six weeks before he asked Tortoise for the money again.

"Please give me one more week," said Tortoise, "I will surely refund your money."

After two weeks, Pig went to Tortoise's home to ask for his money, but Tortoise's wife, Yanrinbo, told Pig that her husband had gone on a trip.

"A trip? He never goes anywhere without

telling me," responded Pig, confused. "Please ask him to come by my home when he returns."

Tortoise by now had stopped going to Pig's home. He avoided Pig as much as he could. He didn't show up for their weekly board game and whenever Pig called out to him in the market, Tortoise would be in a hurry to meet up with a customer. After a while, Tortoise even stopped going to the market.

As time drew closer for the new piglets to be born, Pig became upset with Tortoise. "How can Tortoise do this to me and my family," Pig thought. "He knows we need a new home urgently, yet not only has he not paid back my money, he now hides from me." Pig decided to go to Tortoise's home very early the following morning. He knocked on the door, but there was no response. He knocked harder. He was sure he heard whispers inside the house. Pig knocked even harder.

"Quick," Tortoise whispered to his wife, "Tell him I went out early."

Tortoise ran to the kitchen, folded his hands and feet under him, buried his head under his shell and became like a stone. He popped out his head to ask Yanrinbo to put some peppers on his back. Then he tucked it back in.

"Who is at the door, so early in the morning," Yanrinbo asked.

"Yanrinbo, Good morning. It is Pig. Is Tortoise still asleep?"

"Good morning, Pig. No, Tortoise, left early today," said Yanrinbo as she opened the door.

"Is that true? He left the house even before Cock crowed?" Pig asked suspiciously.

"It's just that he has been working very hard. As you know, we are really in need of money right now," she responded as she walked towards the kitchen. Yanrinbo bent by the huge grinding stone in a corner of the kitchen, looked up at Pig who had walked in after her and said, "Please, come back in the evening. As you can see, I am busy grinding pepper for this afternoon's jollof rice."

Pig looked curiously at the grinding stone and asked, "What happened to the expensive grinder Tortoise bought a few months ago?"

"Err... err, it—it recently started to leak on the sides," she answered.

"Are you sure Tortoise isn't in this house?" Pig

was still suspicious. "Because I'm sure I heard his voice when I was knocking." As Pig was speaking, he was looking carefully around. When he noticed that the back door was ajar, his face turned red. "I bet Tortoise ran out this door when he heard my voice," shouted Pig , as he pushed the door wide open and looked outside.

"No," Yarinbo replied hastily. "The door is usually left open for fresh air. Please lower your voice, you will wake the young ones."

But Pig was now furious. "Tortoise has played me again!" he yelled. In anger, he picked up the grinding stone and threw it with the peppers out the door.

Yanrinbo began to cry.

Pig looked at her and his anger was replaced with shame. "I am sorry, Yanrinbo," he said, "Forgive me. You know the new piglets will soon be born and I desperately need the money Tortoise owes me to build my family a new home." Pig was filled with remorse. "The grinding stone must have fallen among the bushes, let me go and get it. I will ask my wife to bring you some fresh peppers from our garden."

As Pig was about to walk out the back door, Tortoise came into the house through the front door and met them in the kitchen. Tortoise's crafty mind had begun whirring.

"Good morning, my dear friend," he said to Pig with a smile. "I had to leave early this morning to collect a debt. Hope you haven't been waiting for long? I'm glad you are here because I have your money now. I hid it somewhere safe." Tortoise winked secretly at Yanrinbo, and then frowned. "Yanrinbo, where is the grinding stone we keep here?"

"I was just about going to get it from outside when you walked in," said Pig.

"From outside? How did it get outside?" Tortoise asked, looking puzzled at both his wife and Pig.

"I—err," Pig began, "I may have—err…"

"Pig threw the grinding stone out the door," said Yanrinbo.

"He did what?" Tortoise turned to Pig. "You threw the stone out the door?"

"I – err… let me go get it back," said Pig.

"But why?" exclaimed Tortoise as he followed Pig out the back door.

"I... err— I am sorry," said Pig. "Let me just... get it."

"Can you see it?" asked Tortoise. "No, I can't, but it must be around here somewhere. This is the direction I threw it. It was so heavy that I couldn't throw it far," responded Pig.

"The stone is gone," exclaimed Tortoise. "Oh no! Pig, my friend, all my money was in there. What I owed you, what I owed others, your interest, their interest, all my profit; I hid it all in the crack under the stone! Oh no! The stone is gone!"

Yanrinbo began to wail too as she heard her husband lament. Pig was shocked. His legs began to shake and he began to sweat. "Oh, Tortoise, I am sorry. I didn't know. Wait, let me look for it. It must be among the shrubs for sure. It has to be here somewhere." Pig began to sniff around the ground searching for the stone and grunting in sorrow. "The stone should be just about here. I will find it. It must have fallen among the plants. I will find it."

Till this day, Pig sniffs the ground searching for Tortoise's grinding stone.

14

The Slave Sister

A very long time ago, there were three sisters who loved one another dearly. They enjoyed spending time together, working, singing and dancing. The eldest sister, Uyinmwen, always took care of her younger ones, Oghomwen and Oyenmwen, making sure they had their baths and ate their meals on time. She braided their hair, taught them how to knit and sew, and how to sing and dance. The sisters helped one another with their chores and shared everything, including their secrets.

For years, before Oyenmwen was born, the family had hoped for another child. Uyinmwen had longed for another baby sister, particularly as Oghomwen had grown beyond the age that she could carry her around on her back. Oghomwen had also developed her own interests, some of which were different from Uyinmwen's. While Oghomwen liked to play outdoors in the sand or at the stream, Uyinmwen preferred to stay indoors knitting or singing. Uyinmwen yearned for another companion, an in-house play mate. She wanted to have someone else she could retell the favourite parts of the folktales she and the other children were told at the village square, also to sing the folksongs – especially the duets or the call and response songs – when Oghomwen was outside playing. Oghomwen also wanted a younger sister. She wanted a constant outdoor playmate and someone to jump into the stream with her whenever their parents sent them to fetch water. She also didn't want to remain the sole suspect of any broken item in their home.

The day Oyenmwen was born, Uyinmwen and Oghomwen had been full of joy. It was a beautiful morning. The sun was only just rising and a slight wind blew in through the windows as Uyinmwen and Oghomwen gazed at their tiny new sister. Even as they grew up, Uyinmwen and Oghomwen would never forget how innocent and pure their baby sister had looked that morning; how the birds sang in the trees and how the leaves swayed merrily. It had seemed as though nature was joining them in celebrating the newborn.

The sisters often helped their parents on their farm, which was a little distance from their village. They grew many crops, both for sale and for their food. One day, their mother sent them to the farm to get some plantains for dinner. "You girls should hurry up today," she said. "Don't stop to stare at birds or look at flowers. Bring the plantains back quickly so we can start making dinner before sunset."

Uyinmwen and Oyenmwen sang all the way to the farm, while Oghomwen skipped along kicking sand in all directions.

"Oyenmwen, take only a few," said Uyinmwen as she and Oghomwen strapped large bunches of plantain onto their own heads. "I don't want your load to be too heavy."

"Mother will be pleased that we arrived early enough to start off with today's dinner," Uyinmwen said as they headed back home.

Oyenmwen agreed. "I am so hungry. I can't wait to eat Mother's delicious *owo* soup with boiled plantains," she said with a sigh of longing. "I can taste the palm oil, crayfish and smoked fish already."

Oghomwen chuckled. "If you want more than an imaginary taste then you'd better walk a little faster."

Suddenly, they heard a loud blast from the direction of their village.

"Did you hear that?" asked Oyenmwen.

"I heard it," said Oghomwen. "I don't know what it is."

"I heard it too," said Uyinmwen. "Let's hurry."

There came another blast, and then another. The girls began running as fast as their loads would let them, all three very frightened. When they came out of the trees, they could see their village.

What they saw made them scream and throw down their plantains.

"Uyinmwen, is that smoke? Is that fire?" asked Oyenmwen in a trembling voice. "Why are people screaming and running? Uyi...Uyinmwen what is happening?" Oyenmwen was now crying and shaking.

"I don't know," replied Uyinmwen, her voice shaking too. "But I think something bad is happening."

The sisters clung to one another, too frightened to move. As they watched, they saw men on horseback chasing the villagers towards them.

"Our village is under attack!" Uyinmwen cried out. She held on to her sisters and as they ran back in the direction of the farm she said, "Whatever happens, hold on to my hands."

They ran as fast as they could, but people from the village ran even faster. Many ran past them, screaming as they tried to escape the men on horseback who were picking women and children and riding off with them.

The sisters looked around frantically for a place to hide.

"Behind the elephant grass over there", Og-homwen said as she let go of Uyinmwen's hand and headed towards the tall grass. Just as Uyinmwen made to follow Oghomwen, a young injured girl lying in the bush grabbed her wrapper. "Please, help me up," she cried. "Please, help me."

Uyinmwen tried to shake her off. "Let go of my wrapper!" she said. But the girl held on desperately. As Uyinmwen let go of Oyenmwen to help the girl, calling out to Oghomwen as she disappeared into the fields, a rider galloped by and swept Oyenmwen up and onto his horse.

"No! Let me go," Oyenmwen screamed. "Uyinmwen! Help!"

"My sister!" Uyinmwen screamed as she ran after the horse. "My sister! Please, don't take her away." Blinded by her tears, Unyimwen tried to chase the horse. There were other horsemen all round her in the bush and people were screaming. Uyinmwen was still screaming after her sister when she felt herself lifted off the ground by another horse rider.

"My sisters! My sisters!" Uyinmwen cried as she looked back and forth between the elephant grass

Oghomwen had run towards and the direction Oyenmwen had been taken. Amidst the screams and the sound of galloping hooves, she could hear Oyenmwen screaming and calling out for her too. As the horse galloped faster and further away, Uyinmwen cried louder, "My sister, Oyenmwen! Please don't separate us! "Oghomwen, where are you?" Please let me go!" But Unyimwen soon realised that her screaming was futile. She watched helplessly as both the elephant grass and Oyenmwen slowly faded from her sight.

It was a long and tiring ride until they arrived at a village unknown to Uyinmwen. She was dropped off in the village square along with other captured people, young and old. They were not tied, but stern looking men sat on horses, watching them. Uyinmwen looked around for her sister and her parents, but she did not recognise any of the people around her.

"Is that you, Uyinmwen?" a weak voice asked.

Uyinmwen turned and saw it was their neighbour, a young bride who had married just the previous month. She crept to where the woman sat and hugged her, grateful for a familiar face.

"Have you seen my sisters or my parents?" Uyinmwen asked anxiously.

"No, I haven't, I'm sorry," replied the woman sadly. "Have you seen my husband?"

Uyinmwen shook her head. "What happened in the village?" Uyinmwen asked.

The woman sighed. "You know there has been a long-time feud among the seven villages in the region," she said. "I don't know what caused it to get out of hand yesterday, leading to this war. I don't even know which of the villages in the region we are in right now."

Uyinmwen shook her head. "I must find my sisters and my parents," she said as tears fell from her eyes.

"I also need to find my husband," the woman replied. "But who knows where they were taken? I heard that all the men in our village were captured and taken towards the forest."

Uyinmwen and the woman stared off into the distance, lost in their thoughts. As the sky darkened and night fell, they held hands and cried themselves to sleep.

It felt like they had slept for only seconds before a voice barked down at them. "Wake up, all of you!" It was a stern-faced man. Uyinmwen and her neighbour sprang to their feet at once. "You all, fall into groups! Girls, boys, women, quickly!"

Uyinmwen's eyes welled with tears as she was separated from the only person she knew in that strange place. She joined a group of teenage girls and they were led to a huge compound with many huts.

"Welcome to your new home," an elderly woman said with a smile. "Here, you will be trained to serve in the inner courts of the palace."

The days went by, rolling into weeks, months and then years. The elderly woman had taken a special liking to Uyinmwen over the years and adopted her as her own daughter. Uyinmwen settled into her new life and matured into a very beautiful young woman.

One day, the queen mother held a royal banquet for her son, the king, to which she invited all the maidens in the village. The elderly woman helped Uyinmwen get dressed. "You look lovely my daughter," she said to Uyinmwen as she walked with her towards the palace. It was truly a grand event. The decorations were spectacular, the food and drinks were abundant and the music was delightful. The maidens chatted in groups while the king walked gracefully around, welcoming them.

While dancing, one of the maidens stepped on her wrapper and tripped. The other young women laughed, but Uyinmwen walked to her and helped her up. "Are you alright?" she asked. The young woman nodded with embarrassment and thanked Uyinmwen.

The king saw this kind gesture and walked up to the ladies. He was immediately struck by Uyinmwen's warm smile and beauty.

"Would you care to dance with me?" he asked politely. Uyinmwen gave a shy nod and they both began to dance. Uyinmwen had always been a good dancer, and the young king was as well. They made a dashing couple on the dance floor.

The queen mother watched from a distance with a smile on her face. She was very pleased with her son's choice.

She turned to her lady-in-waiting with a sparkle in her eyes. "Find out whose daughter that is," she said. "We might be having a royal wedding soon."

Indeed, there soon was a royal wedding as

Ezeilekhea, the king, and Uyinmwen got married. It was a magnificent occasion that was talked about for a long time even in the neighbouring villages.

Uyinmwen settled into yet another new life as queen. But as time went by she became a rather vain and arrogant queen.

Oyenmwen, on the other hand, had been carried off to a distant village where she was raised by a very poor family. Things got so bad for them that they had to send Oyenmwen off to another village to work as a servant. This village happened to be the one in which Uyinmwen was now queen.

Oyenmwen had become a skinny young girl with a very sad face. She missed her parents and sisters dearly, in spite of the time that had passed. She often remembered the comfort of their home and the good food they had to eat. She missed the love and care of her family.

When she arrived at Uyinmwen's village, she was taken to work on the outer courts of the palace. Early every morning, she would wake up to sweep the palace grounds and its surroundings. Many times she would overhear the other servants talk about the queen. Oyenmwen looked forward to getting a glimpse of her someday.

One day, the queen took her usual evening walk around the palace. But this time she went closer to the servant's quarters than she had ever done before to admire some blooming flowers. Oyenmwen was sitting in a corner with some other servants eating their supper when they saw the queen walk by.

"I know that face," Oyenmwen said to herself. "I know that face, but it can't be," she said aloud.

"Shhh!" said the other servants. "Please don't make the queen look our way."

Just then the queen turned in their direction. This time there was no doubt; Oyenmwen saw that it was indeed Uyinmwen, her older sister. Oyenmwen's eyes widened and her jaw dropped. She had dreamed of this moment every night since they had been separated. The hope of seeing her family again had kept her strong through the hard times she had faced over the years. She stood and took a step forward.

"Where do you think you are going?" one of the other servants snapped. "Don't you know that we are to stay out of sight whenever the queen is in the outer courts?"

"It's Uyi...It's Uyinmwen" Oyenmwen replied, and she ran towards the queen with tears streaming down her cheeks.

"Wait! Don't!" whispered the servant.

As Oyenmwen was about to call out to her sister, she was cut off by the royal guards.

"And where do you think you are going?" demanded one of them.

"I... em—"

"What is going on there?" asked the queen.

"Nothing at all," replied the guard. "It's just one of the maids that seems to be overstepping her bounds."

"Maid? What maid thinks she can come this close to me?" demanded the queen.

"Move aside and let me see her!" she ordered. By this time, Oyenmwen was shaking and bowed her head as the queen looked scornfully at her. Uyinmwen looked at the haggard girl and said, "How dare you approach me?"

"I... I—"

"Be quiet!" commanded Uyinmwen. She looked

Oyenmwen from head to toe and said, "You will be punished for this." Then she walked away.

The queen sent for the head-maid and said to her, "Hence forth, give that maid that dared to come into my presence twice as much work to do, and let her eat only after all the other servants have eaten."

Oyenmwen could not believe her older sister had not recognised her. She was devastated. This was not the reunion she had dreamt of all these years. She cried herself to sleep that night, and for many nights after. She even began to doubt if the queen was truly her sister, Uyinmwen. The other servants made fun of her endlessly, and wherever she went, their mocking giggles and stifled laughter followed her. Oyenmwen bore all of this. She continued to do her chores diligently and ate what was left after all the palace servants had eaten. But she had begun to sing a song to herself as she did her chores, a slow sad song that came from her heart; a song of her sorrows.

One day, while Oyenmwen was washing a basket of clothes, the queen mother overheard her tearful singing:

Iye ima gie ima ugbo	Our mother sent us to the farm
Erha ima gie ima ugbo	Our father sent us to the farm
Yayatiya	Drum beat
Okuo ke khẹn ima vbe ode ugbo	We were caught in the war on our way
Okuo ke khẹn ima eheha	The three of us were caught in the war
Yayatiya	Drum beat
A kien ime ne udo, udo ma dee	I was offered to the east, but they didn't want me
A khien ime ne eka, eka ma de	I was offered to the west, but they turned me back
Yayatiya	Drum beat
Agbon ghi ma Uyinmwen ne	When Uyinmwen started to live in luxury
Te o ghi de ovbieyere	She bought her mother's child
Te o ghi de ovbierhare	She bought her father's child
Yayatiya	Drum beat
Agbon ghi maa Uyinmwen ne	When Uyinmwen started to live in luxury
Te o ghi mu iku nu me	She gave me peels of yam and leftovers
Vbe be a mu uku ne ewe	Just as they are given to goats
Yayatiya	Drum beat
Agbon ghi maa Uyinmwen ne	When Uyinmwen started to live in luxury
Te o ghi mu owo sin me	She treated me like filth

Vbe ne a mu owo sin erhan	*Just as filth is disgusting*
Yayatiya	*Drum beat*
Uyinmwen ne ovbieye mwe	*Uyinmwen my mother's child*
Uyinmwen ne ovbierha mwe	*Uyinmwen my father's child*
Yayatiya	*Drum beat*
Uyinmwen ne ovbieye mwe	*Uyinmwen my mother's child*
Uyinmwen ne ovbierha mwe	*Uyinmwen my father's child*
Yayatiya	*Drum beat*

The queen mother was surprised. "Could this be true?" she wondered. She felt the pain from the sad young girl and her heart troubled her till she decided to do some fact-finding. She paid a visit to the elderly woman whom she believed to be Uyinmwen's mother and told her about the young girl's song.

"It must be true," the elderly woman said. She went on to tell the queen mother all Uyinmwen had shared with her about her real family and their separation after the war. The queen mother returned to the palace lost in thought.

The following day, the queen mother went to see the king and queen. "It's about the maid being punished by the queen," she said.

"What maid?" asked Uyinmwen.

"The one who tried to approach you some months ago," the queen mother said.

"Oh, I had forgotten about her." Uyinmwen said. "What has that girl done this time? Was she rude to you? Tell me so I can have her punished even more."

The queen mother shook her head gently and said, "Nothing actually, she hasn't done anything. But, please, come with me."

The queen mother led Ezeilekhea and Uyinmwen to a window in one of the palace rooms and asked them to listen closely to the words of the maid's song.

Uyinmwen could not believe her ears.

"It can't be," she whispered as tears welled up in her eyes and rolled down her cheeks. She turned to her husband. "I would recognise Oyenmwen's voice anywhere. I have been hoping all these years to hear her sing again." She began to sob.

Oyenmwen carried on with her chores and sang her sorrowful song, unaware that she was being observed from above. As she sang, she raised her head once and Uyinmwen saw her face clearly for the first time. Her heart broke. Certainly, the sad face and ragged body she saw were those of her long lost baby sister, Oyenmwen.

"I have been so cruel to her," Uyinmwen said as she cried even harder. "Will she ever forgive me?"

"Well, it's never too late to do the right thing," the king said to her.

With the king's words resounding in her ears, Uyinmwen ran out of the palace into the outer courts, crying as she called out to her sister, "Oyenmwen! Oyenmwen, my sister, at last, I have found a member of my family. I am so sorry. Please, forgive me..."

15

Tortoise and the Gourd of Wisdom

One evening, Tortoise was sitting under a tree eating sugar canes and feeling generally pleased with himself when Pig and Deer walked by, talking animatedly.

"Owl will surely know what to do," Pig said to Deer. "I think we need to consult him."

"Here we go again," Tortoise said to himself, rolling his eyes. "Owl! Owl! Owl! Whenever any animal needs advice they go to Owl, as if he is the only one in the world with wisdom. I want to be the only one in the world that knows about everything. When I solve problems or share great ideas, I will charge a huge fee. I will become the richest and most sought-after being in the world... But how do I go about getting all this wisdom?"

Tortoise mulled this over for many hours and finally came up with an idea: he would begin by getting the wisdom of all the other animals.

He went to Giraffe and said, "I heard of a place, not so far away, where wisdom can be multiplied."

Giraffe seemed intrigued. "Really? How does that work?"

"Place your wisdom in this gourd so I can take it there, and when I return it, you will be twice as wise as you are now."

Giraffe gave Tortoise all his wisdom.

Tortoise went to Antelope and said, "I heard of a place, not so far away, where wisdom can be multiplied. Place your wisdom in this gourd so I can take it there, and when I return it, you will be twice as wise as you are now."

Antelope thought about it and agreed. He placed his wisdom in the gourd.

Tortoise went to Fox and said, "I heard of a place, not so far away, where wisdom can be multiplied. Place your wisdom in this gourd so I can take it there, and when I return it, you will be twice as wise as you are now."

Fox began to laugh. "Tortoise, is this one of your tricks? Tell me where the place is so I can go and multiply my wisdom myself."

"If you think, this is a trick, then you will be disappointed when you find you are the dumbest in the whole kingdom," Tortoise said to Fox. "You may never get another chance to be wiser."

"You will surely pay dearly if this is a trick," Fox said to Tortoise, as he placed his wisdom in the gourd.

Tortoise next went to Owl and told him the same thing he'd told the other animals.

"Tortoise, I have never heard of such a place," Owl said.

"That's because you don't know everything, Owl. Imagine how much more you would be able to help the animals solve their problems if you became wiser than you already are."

Owl thought for a little while and said, "Okay, Tortoise, you can have half of my wisdom. I will hold on to the other half till you return."

Tortoise frowned slightly, but then he accepted half of Owl's wisdom. "I will still be far wiser than Owl with all the wisdom I will gather," he said to himself.

One after the other, Tortoise met the animals and told them about the place where wisdom could be doubled. Many believed him and gave him all their wisdom. Tortoise only shrugged and told those who didn't believe the same thing he had told Fox: "If you think this is a trick, then you will be disappointed when you find you are the dumbest in the whole kingdom. You may never get another chance to be wiser." The animals succumbed and gave Tortoise their wisdom.

After gathering the wisdom of all the animals, Tortoise was happy that he had more wisdom than all of the animals put together. He began to search for the safest place to hide his gourd of wisdom.

There was a sacred tree in the forest that had existed long before the animals. It was the tallest and biggest tree in all the kingdom, and many believed it would never die or be felled. It was at the top of this tree that Tortoise decided to hide his gourd of wisdom.

He tied a rope round the gourd and hung it over his neck and in front of his chest. Tortoise wanted to keep his eyes on the gourd as he climbed up the tree. He grabbed the tree with both hands and tried to push himself up, but each time he slid back down. Tortoise tried again and again to climb up the tree, but he kept sliding down. "Maybe my hands are slippery," he said to himself as he rubbed some earth on them. But even after this he kept sliding down. "Maybe the trunk is slippery," he said, as he rubbed some earth on the trunk. But again, he slid down.

Tortoise sat under the tree to think of a solution. "I have more wisdom than any animal in this kingdom," he said. "If I can't climb this tree then no other animal can."

But just then, Owl, who had seen Tortoise trying to climb up the tree, called out, "Tortoise, you have to toss the gourd to your back if you want to climb up that tree!"

"What did you say?" asked Tortoise.

"It's the gourd hanging down your chest that is making you slide down," Owl said. "Hang it on your back so that you can climb up the tree without any obstacle."

Tortoise thanked Owl for his advice. He hung the gourd securely on his back and climbed up the tree easily.

When Tortoise got to the top of the tree, it dawned on him that even with all the wisdom he had gathered, he still needed advice to climb up the tree. Now remorseful, Tortoise went back to all the animals and returned the wisdom he had collected from them.

He had learnt that no single being can have the entire world's wisdom, and that knowledge is meant to be shared and spread.

Music[1]

A o m'ẹ́rin j'ọba
From "How Lion became the King
of the Jungle".

Nne e Nne e
From "The Broken Pot".

Ma d'ènìyàn
From "Why Monkeys Live in the Forest".

Asín t'òhun t'ǫ̀kẹ́rẹ́
From "Why Tortoise has a Small Nose."

157

Etok ebok
From "Monkey and the Couple's Child".

Yayatiya
From "The Slave Sister".

About the Author

Efe Farinre (née Edebiri) is the founder of Linking Hands Foundation (LHF), a non-governmental organisation focused on children's education, health and values. An advocate for the total well-being of children, Efe's work has been featured in the Nigerian press. She had her secondary school education at Queen's College, Yaba, Lagos, Nigeria and graduated from the University of Lagos, Nigeria with a B.Sc. in Chemical Engineering. Efe also holds an M.Sc. in International Purchasing and

Supply Chain Management from *Audencia Nantes Ecole de Management*, Nantes, France. Born in Lagos, Nigeria, Efe has lived on three continents, and speaks English, Yoruba and French. She currently resides in her place of birth with her husband and children. A burning desire ignited by her children, to preserve a vital part of her oral cultural heritage, inspired Efe to create *Folktales are Forever*.

18764007R00094

Printed in Poland
by Amazon Fulfillment
Poland Sp. z o.o., Wrocław